Ain't No Sunshine

Ain't No Sunshine

Candice Dow

KENSINGTON PUBLISHING CORP.
http://www.kensingtonbooks.com

DAFINA BOOKS are published by

Kensington Publishing Corp.
850 Third Avenue
New York, NY 10022

All Kensington titles, imprints and distributed lines are available at special quantity discounts for bulk purchases for sales promotion, premiums, fund-raising, educational or institutional use.

Special book excerpts or customized printings can also be created to fit specific needs. For details, write or phone the office of the Kensington Special Sales Manager: Kensington Publishing Corp., 850 Third Avenue, New York, NY 10022. Attn. Special Sales Department. Phone: 1-800-221-2647.

Dafina Books and the Dafina logo Reg. U.S. Pat. & TM Off.

ISBN 0-7582-1055-8

First Kensington Trade Paperback Printing: June 2006
10 9 8 7 6 5 4 3 2 1

Printed in the United States of America

Acknowledgments

I would like to thank God for allowing me to use this creative gift. I am truly humbled by His blessings. To my family and friends, thank you for always having my back. Your love keeps me pressing on. To all of my fellow authors who have guided me along the way, I greatly appreciate your words of wisdom. Brenda L. Thomas, you are an angel. Thank you for being so unselfish with your knowledge. Carl Weber, thanks for taking me under your wing and making me feel like family. Victoria Christopher-Murray, for always wearing a smile.

Special thanks to Radience Pittman, Robilyn Heath, Kwame Alexander, Earl Cox, Books That Click, Shunda Leigh, Booking Matters. Pamela Walker-Williams, PageTurner.net, Heather Covington, *Disilgold Magazine*. A huge shout out to all of the book clubs! Thanks for holding us down. RAWSISTAZ, Women of Distinction, Peoplewholovegoodbooks, Nubian Sistas Book Club, RSVP Book Club, APOOO Book Club, and so many more.

My agent, Audra Barrett; my editor, Karen Thomas, and the entire Kensington staff, you are the best.

Most of all, I would like to thank the readers for allowing me to touch your life, because you have truly touched mine. And for anyone I may have forgotten, thank you so, so much for sharing my dream.

PROLOGUE

As she'd done three nights a week for the past two years, Laila pulled her small roller bag from under the bed. She removed the freezer bag full of the previous night's tips and dumped the crumpled money into the chest. She repacked her bag; makeup, platform heels, and a sexy costume. She slipped on her tennis shoes and pulled her long silky ponytail through her black Nike cap. She fluffed pillows under the bedcovers to create the illusion of a human lying inside. Her roommate's eyes were glued to the television, unfazed by the routine. Laila reminded her, "You know you have to hand me my bag."

Her roommate nodded. Laila tied her T-shirt in the back and exposed her belly ring. She folded her body up on the window seat and swung her legs out of the window, ducking her head out simultaneously. Her roommate dragged the bag over to the window and lowered it over the sill. In one swooping motion, she caught it and tossed it into the garden below. Laila crawled from the flat awning of the two-level group home. Her roommate folded a towel into the crack of the window sill, so Laila could easily reenter.

Laila climbed down onto the back porch and peeped into the small kitchen window. The staff member on duty sat smooching on the couch with her boyfriend. Laila shook her head. They were both out of order, but Laila knew she was safe until six the next morning. She darted out of the backyard, bag in tow. She reached into her tight denim shorts to retrieve her cell phone to disable the silent option. Her slim, muscular legs galloped through her North Miami neighborhood. To avoid recognition, as if neighbors didn't already know her routine, she hung her head low.

A horn blew and startled her. It was a fellow dancer, Gina. She pulled over for Laila to hop in her convertible Celica. Huge earrings dangled from her ears. False eyelashes and other makeup covered the pain of years of bodily misuse. Laila often wondered why Gina had been in the game for over ten years. Laila wanted more, though a real future seemed unattainable. She got in the car.

She kissed Gina's cheek. "Hey girl . . ."

Gina tapped her flamboyant claws on her steering wheel. "What's up, Ms. Lady?"

"Nothing, I didn't even feel like coming tonight."

The anticipation that once inspired her each night had dissipated. After more than fifty men and practically every non-terminal sexually transmitted disease, Laila was exhausted.

Gina rolled her eyes. "You never do."

Gina laughed. Though Laila was a natural beauty, Gina was infamous for making her feel self-conscious. Laila pulled her cap off and raised her eyebrows, "What?"

"You look like a damn ghost with all that black."

Laila smirked. Gina tickled her chin. "Just fucking with you, baby girl."

Laila shrugged her shoulders, but inside she was furious. Gina made light of her charcoal skin color almost daily, as if it were a handicap. They pulled up to the club a few minutes later.

When they got inside, Laila ripped her clothes off. She put on a pink patent leather costume and tied a huge pink bow around her ponytail. As she decorated her eyes, Gina came over to the cloudy mirror. "That's too pink for you."

Laila huffed, "It'll do for tonight."

Gina rolled her eyes. "If you say so. You should put on some blush."

Laila's fetish was eye makeup, beyond that she kept it simple. Her high cheekbones and perfect heart-shaped lips gave the illusion of a fully made-up stage face. She shook her head, "That's okay. I'm cool."

"Laila, you look like you're thirteen. You need more makeup."

The stage manager rushed in, "Quiet Storm, you're up next."

Laila ignored Gina and nodded at the manager. She stepped into a pair of clear plastic platform sandals. Gina walked away. "You can't tell these young girls nothing."

Laila rushed out of the dressing room. The DJ mixed her music. She stormed on stage. Smoke surrounded her, as she posed at the back of the stage. The crowd howled. Silver glitter sparkled on her radiant charcoal skin under the fluorescent lights. She batted her fake eyelashes. To end the suspense, she strutted to the front of the stage: her attitude, demanding. Her motion, intensive. As she danced, she stared into the eyes of over twenty men like those who had destroyed her innocence. She unsnapped her top. Intoxicated men leaned on the edge of the stage, drooling as if her age wasn't evident by the perkiness of her young breasts. They tossed money on the stage. Some tucked it into her G-string. Her angelic smile thanked her patrons, as her ten-second count began. On her knees, she clapped her thighs, gathering the scattered tips between her legs. She blew kisses. On the floor, she rolled backwards off the stage. The storm was over.

As always, she changed into another costume and returned to work the crowd. As she bounced on one of the regulars, she made eye contact with an unfamiliar face over his shoulder. She smiled. He nodded. She reached for his hand and intertwined her fingers in his. They beamed at each other. The intensity distracted her rhythm. Slowly, she climbed off the man she was entertaining. She stared deeply into the eyes of the stranger, as she seductively straddled him. She began to twirl her twenty-eight inch waist.

.As she gyrated on him, he sipped his drink. He put money in her G-string, but appeared unimpressed by her performance. Her sexuality being her pride, she ground her hips vigorously, hoping to invoke a reaction from the dark, handsome man. He continued to sip his drink, as if he was watching a television show. Feeling useless, she neutralized her efforts. Finally he asked, "How old are you?"

"Twenty."

He chuckled. "You ain't no damn twenty."

She pumped harder. "Yes, I am."

"You look like a baby. Tell me the truth."

She redirected the question. "How old are you?"

"I'm twenty-five."

The lack of hair on his face made him look much younger. Laila curled her lips. "Yeah, sure."

He smiled. "What's your name?"

"Laila."

"A pretty name for a pretty girl."

She smirked. In her mind, compliments were just pathways to the panties, for the mirror never reflected the beauty that so many men raved about.

He ran his forefinger down the side of her delicate face. "Laila, why you in here?"

She ignored him. He asked again. "Why you selling your body like this?"

She didn't respond. He pried further. "How long you been doing this?"

She took a deep breath, "Too long."

He sat up. His mouth grazed her lips. His eyes pierced into her eyes. "You tired?"

She swallowed his question. It swirled around in her stomach. She felt sick. Sick and tired. His eyes demanded a response. Finally, she nodded. He pulled a business card from his jacket. "Call me."

He took another sip and tapped her thighs. "All right. I'm about to go."

She stood up. Other men summoned her, but she staggered slightly and read the business card. David Dubois. No way could a realtor want any more than sex. The chill from his touch still tingled. She was baffled. Most men stated their intentions from the door. Mr. Dubois seemed more compassionate. As if common sense smacked her, she snapped out of her daze and plowed through the crowd to catch him.

She rushed up behind him, "Hey."

He smiled. "What's up?"

Although she'd promised she wasn't going to sleep with another man at the club, she put her hands on her hips. "Whatchu want?"

He frowned. "Whatchu talking about?"

"What do you want from me?"

He chuckled. "I want to get your young ass out of this club."

She stepped closer. "And what are you going to do with me after you get me out of here?"

He dropped his head and sighed. "Take you home."

She tugged on his jacket and batted her eyes. "But, I don't have a home."

"Well I'll find you one."

She smirked. "Really?"

"You ready?"

She nodded. "Lemme get my stuff."

He stood at the door, awaiting her return and wondering how a girl that young ended up a veteran in such a dangerous game.

She darted up the stairs and sighed. "Ready."

They sat in the car, but he didn't put the key in the ignition. "Laila, where you live?"

She smiled. "I told you. I don't have a home."

He started the car. They hopped on Interstate 95, heading north. Assuming they were headed to a Fort Lauderdale hotel, Laila sat quietly. When they passed Exit 26, she began to get nervous. She always took note of her surroundings. The ride had been way too long. It was outside of her territory. The Fort Lauderdale airport was her cut-off. Laila's heart pounded. She found the courage to ask, "Where we going?"

"I'm taking you to my house."

In between deep breaths, she asked, "Where do you live?"

"In Coconut Creek."

Still afraid, she asked, "How far is it? Do you want to just get a hotel?"

He chuckled. "I'm not trying to sleep with you. I'm taking your young ass to the Department of Social Services in the morning."

Laila frowned, "What? Why are you so concerned? Either you're interested or you're not. I can catch a cab."

He chuckled. "I didn't take you out of that club because I was interested. I felt sorry for you. And damn if you can catch a cab from all the way out here."

Offended that he saw her as a charity project, she huffed, "Take me home then."

He chuckled. "I thought you didn't have a home."

Finally, he exited on Copans Road and explained, "I live right down here on the left."

Keeping mental notes of her whereabouts, Laila nodded. They pulled into the Centura Parc development.

"Do you live in this development?"

She pulled out her cell phone and sent Gina a text message. DAVID DUBOIS. COCONUT CREEK. 95 NORTH. EXIT 36. LEFT INTO CENTURA PARC.

A part of Laila was nervous about typing in her phone, but as much as he seemed trustworthy, she had to be cautious. When they reached his house, she asked, "Is this your house?"

He nodded. She sent Gina the exact address as they got out and walked to the door of his single family stucco home.

When they stepped in, Laila looked around in awe. Her phone beeped. Gina responded. UR YOUNG ASS IS TRYNA DIE.

Laila curled her lips. Dying was the least of her worries.

As her eyes took a quick tour of his home, she couldn't imagine a black man living so well. She wanted him to want her. Maybe he could be her way out.

He jingled his keys. "So do you have a home or what?"

"It all depends on what you call a home."

He sat on the steps across from the front door, as if they were leaving at any moment. "C'mon. Stop playin'."

Laila walked up and stood between his legs. David admired her beauty, and tried to resist the temptation. The intellect in her words and the maturity in her voice baffled him. After a few minutes of conversation, he asked, "How old are you for real?"

She felt his sincerity. She sighed and slouched down beside him. "Seventeen."

He was silent momentarily. "Seventeen, huh?"

That had never discouraged any of the other perverts. Regretting her fumble, she laughed. "Sike. I'm twenty."

"How did a seventeen-year-old start strippin'?"

She corrected him. "Dancing."

"Whatever you want to call it. How did you start?"

She leaned her head on his shoulder. "A hard life."

He patted her knee. "Tell me about it."

"It's a long story."

He looked at his watch. "I got time."

She stumbled over some of the major details, but the life she loved to hide spilled from her mouth. She spoke in the third person, her way of removing herself from reality.

"A lady checked into a hospital with a false name. She gave birth to a little girl. A day later, she disappeared. The baby's picture was all over the news. No one came forth to help. No one seemed to know who the masked lady was. No one wanted to adopt the baby, because it was believed that she was born addicted."

She stepped out of her narrative and chuckled, "Who wants a crack baby, right?"

Entranced by the story, he didn't respond. "Needless to say, the baby goes into the foster care system. Throughout her life, she's shifted from home to home, over a dozen homes by the age of fifteen. One day she gets it." She looked at David, as if he'd know what *it* was. She shook her head. "Nobody gives a fuck."

She took a deep breath. "Nobody! You gotta make your own way."

He rubbed her knee. Her eyes lowered, "And she gave birth to Quiet Storm."

He brushed her hair back. "You deserve a better life."

She smirked. "I've learned to accept the cards I'm dealt. I don't trip anymore."

He fought the desire, but he lost the battle. He kissed her soft lips. She responded. She wrapped her arms around his neck. He stopped mid-kiss. "I'm not tryna sleep with you tonight."

Now aroused, Laila nibbled his ear. "It's okay. I want you."

"Not until you're eighteen."

"I'll be eighteen in two weeks."

He pulled away from her. She whispered. "C'mon. No one will know."

David wanted Laila as much as she wanted him, but he wanted more from her than most men. He got up and walked into the kitchen. Laila remained on the steps. She felt rejected. He returned with a crinkled portrait of a schoolgirl. Two long braids with ribbons on the end hung to the middle of her chest. The picture seemed gloomy, as if a cloud of sadness surrounded the girl. She frowned.

"Who's this?"

"A picture of my mother."

Laila nodded. "Okay . . ."

"You look like her."

The girl in the picture was far more attractive than Laila could ever imagine herself being. Slightly flattered, she smiled and nodded.

He continued, "Yeah, she died giving birth to me."

"Damn. That's pretty sad. How old is she in this picture?"

"She's probably fourteen. She had me when she was sixteen."

"Who raised you?"

"My father. He's a good man. He raised me by hisself."

They both sat silently. He thought about the mother he never knew. Laila wondered why no one cared enough to step in and raise her. Two thriving plants with missing roots, they related.

"Laila, you're a cool ass young girl." He took a deep breath. "It's something about you." He rubbed her leg. "I'm not even trying to hop in the bed with you. I just want you to get out of that club and get yourself together." He paused. "And I'm going to help you."

Laila felt more valuable than the sex toy role she'd succumbed to. Whether or not his promise was sincere, it cracked Laila's rugged shell. Her eyes watered. "You're so sweet."

They hugged and Laila was certain she'd found someone to depend on.

CHAPTER 1

His large hands pressed tightly around my neck. My tongue thrust. Saliva rolled from the corner of my mouth.

As if divine intervention pried his fingers from my neck, he let go. Then, he smacked me. He stood at the foot of the bed. "Bitch, you think I'm crazy?"

Too weak to move, I lay on the blood-soiled sheets, balled in a knot. I tried to shake my head. As if my response enraged him, he jumped on the bed and straddled me. With the force of a bull, he threw repeated blows to my head. Finally, the tears he awaited began to flow. I cried. "David . . . I . . ."

Sweat rolled profusely from his forehead. Sprinkles of his alcohol-contaminated saliva splashed on my face, as he spat out, "Who you fucking?"

I shook my head.

"Why the fuck you using birth control?"

I stuttered, "I . . . I didn't. I . . . I . . ."

He smacked me, "You's a weak bitch!"

He wrapped my hair around his hand and pounded my head against the headboard like a rag doll. "You got me thinking we're trying, and you fucking playing games."

I pleaded, "I . . ."

With his fingers still intertwined in my hair, he stood up. My head dangled from the king-sized bed. He yanked me. My naked body thumped on the floor. He began dragging me. I tried to crawl, but he pulled faster. The carpet scraped against my bare breast. Long strands of hair ripped from my scalp. Suddenly, my body tumbled down the stairs like a wagon in tow.

The full moon beamed through the large window in the foyer. I wished upon a star. Just as I attempted to escape the reality, his size 13 boot smashed against my chest. "Bitch, clean up this house."

I lay facedown on the ceramic tile at the front door. He stomped in circles around me. He yelled, "All I try to do for your sorry ass."

He mumbled to himself. "Sorry bitch." He chuckled. "After fucking the whole city, I guess she can't hold no babies." He bobbed his head from side to side.

After four miscarriages, you'd think he would sympathize. I pleaded for his compassion. How could I bear the pain of losing another baby?

He kneeled down and asked, "When was you gonna tell me you was on the pill?"

I cried, "I don't know."

He rubbed my sore face. "Just tell me the truth."

The bastard grabbed my bloody face in his hands. He kissed me. He whispered in my ear, "Don't bullshit me. I'll kill you before I let you make a fool of me. You know that. Right?"

I nodded. He dropped my head and walked into the kitchen. I watched him move. He opened another fifth of Bacardi Gold, the ammunition of his fury.

He took a sip. "Laila, clean this shit up."

Knowing that lying there would only enrage him again, I rose on my arms. I fell back to the floor. I whimpered, "David . . . I . . ."

His temper slowly crept back, and he shouted, "Get all this shit off the floor!"

Too frightened to submit to my exhaustion, I hopped up. My body swayed. I searched for strength, enough to kill the tar-colored man standing before me. Instead, my heart cried for him. All he wanted was a child of his own and the woman he loved was fruitless.

CHAPTER 2

Twenty minutes of my daily preparation was devoted to covering scratches and scars. As I stood in the bathroom patting under my eyes with concealer, David walked in.

In the mirror I watched him walk behind me. As if he was sleep walking, he stumbled over to the toilet. He yawned. As if he'd exerted all his energy fighting me, he appeared to sway back and forth while he used the toilet. I didn't speak, because I was angry. He probably didn't speak because he hadn't noticed me standing there.

It bothered me that I wasn't sure to whom I should direct my anger. Was I angry with myself for letting my birth control pills slip from my purse? Was I angry because this man had a temper like lighting fluid? Or more important, was I angry that I had no other option?

To avoid confrontation, I said, "Good morning."

He staggered around and stood behind me. Though he mugged, I smiled. Hoping his sober state would be a cause for a better morning, I turned slightly to face him. "Hey, baby."

He rubbed his eyes. "Hey, baby."

I exhaled. The tension that followed the morning after we fought always made me antsy. I never knew if the fight was over or not. So, I always prayed. I always observed his actions. What would he do? What would he say?

He stumbled to the sink next to me and began to wash his hands. I glanced down at his swollen knuckles and winced. He looked at me in the mirror. I smiled. He stared and said, "Your skin is so perfect."

That was his way of admiring how fast I healed. I nodded. He lifted my hair and kissed my neck. "Black is so beautiful."

As I watched the marks miraculously disappear, I grew to value the gift of dark skin. I pulled out my lip gloss, and David snatched it from my hand.

As if the sight of makeup disgusted him, he tilted his head and frowned. "Why you wear that stuff?"

I shrugged my shoulders. "I don't know."

He grazed my face with his abusive hands. "You look better plain."

If you weren't whipping my ass, then I wouldn't need makeup. I nodded. "I know."

I didn't fight for the gloss. Instead, I threw my makeup in my small case. As I bent over to stow it underneath the sink, he pinched my butt and walked out. "That a girl."

I watched his back exit the bathroom. *That a girl.* Did he really think I was his child?

I twisted my ponytail and pinned it up into a bun. My hyperventilating began as I walked from the bathroom. Would today be a good day? What could I do not to piss him off? How could I make him happy?

I looked at the source of my anxiety. He nodded his head. "That's the way I like you. Just like that."

I smirked. "Thanks."

He stood in the middle of the bedroom floor, forcing me to walk around him. A permanent roadblock. With my heart beating a mile a minute, I slipped into my scrubs. I needed to breathe. When he realized I was done getting ready, he yawned and sat on the bed. "Oh yeah, Happy New Year, baby."

I grabbed my keys from the armoire. "You too . . ."

He flipped the channels of the TV. "Shit is gonna be different this year."

I ignored the same resolution I'd heard three years in a row. As I headed out the bedroom door, he reached out for me. I walked up to him. He wrapped his arms around my waist. "I'm sorry."

Hoping to ease my own panic, I stroked his head and closed my eyes. "I know, baby."

As much as I hated our fights, I knew he meant no harm. He just didn't know how to express himself. I pushed his head closer to me. As he rested his head on my belly, this vulnerable moment told me that he needed me as much as I needed him. We were silent. Though he hadn't asked for it, I forgave him.

As if he heard my heart, he promised. "No fighting. No drinking. This is our year."

He lifted my shirt and landed kisses near the womb too weak to grant him his wish. I tried to explain, "David, I'm sorry for . . ."

He reached up and covered my mouth. "Shhh . . ."

How could alcohol turn such a caring man into a crazy animal? I tucked my bottom lip in and took a deep breath. Why did I trust a man who had beaten me for four years? I kissed the forehead of the only person on whom I could depend. "I love you so much."

He stood up and hugged me. "I know, baby."

I grabbed the ugly black mules that I wear to work and slid my feet into them. David lay back in the bed with his hands behind his head. He watched me move, admiration in his eyes. "I hate to see you leave the house."

In an effort to avoid a debate about me working, I rushed out of the house. I sat in the car and took deep breaths before pulling off. The pond across from our house was a part of my calming ritual. I looked out at the pond and imagined one day taking my kids for a walk there. Daydreaming has always been my way to escape. I snapped out of it and started my car.

My job was no more than fifteen minutes away. I traveled the same way every day. All that I needed was on my way. Wal-Mart. Publix. Marshalls. Pompano Citi Center Mall. David checked my mileage so frequently that everything I needed had to be done in the area that covered Copans Road, to Florida A1A, to Atlantic Boulevard. Trapped in a cage in suburbia. His efforts to keep me as far away from the alluring streets of Miami was all for my sake. So he claimed.

Often, mixed emotions filled my head on my short drive to work. *You can make it on your own if you start dancing again. You should leave that crazy bastard.* Then, reality settled in. *He will find my ass.* I shook my head as I pulled into the strip mall.

I sighed. *Freid Chiropractic Center.* The same emotions came over me each time I saw the sign. Peace. Gratitude. If it had not been for Dr. Freid offering me this job, where would I be? I often wondered.

He was a sweetheart for no reason at all. He gave me a chance when I had no experience and he didn't ask for anything in return. Everyone else I had ever trusted took a piece of me in return for what they offered. Not Dr. Freid. I came to his office two years ago with a back injury. He laid me on the table and performed miraculous "cracking," as my ignorance labeled it at that time. The pain seemed to diminish with each visit. The relief left me longing to know more about chiropractic care. After each appointment, I would ask questions. Dr. Freid would allow me as much time as I needed to explain everything. He was passionate about his work and my curiosity made him happy. One day, he offered me a job. Although I was apprehensive, I accepted. Of course, I was accused of fucking my way into a job. David fought me every step of the way, but it was the one thing I was determined not to let him control. Finally, he surrendered. Our fighting increased, but nine hours a day out of his sight was worth every battle. This was my daily antidepressant.

As always, I arrived thirty minutes before everyone else. Just to have coffee, relax, and imagine a life without pain. A girl can dream, can't she?

When the receptionist, Jodi, came in she yelled to the back, "Happy New Year, Laila!"

I strolled to the front of the office, holding my coffee cup close to my swollen lip. "Same to you, Jodi."

She looked at me strangely. I smiled, "Do we have a busy day?"

Without taking her eyes off me, she shook her head. "I don't think so."

She logged on the computer. "It looks like the morning is pretty light. I guess most people are hung over from last night."

I sighed and felt a little sad. My New Year's Eve was stripped away from me because of a mere slipup. I had come down the stairs wearing a black strapless knee-length dress and strappy sandals. My hair was blown out straight. I waltzed into the kitchen, as we had planned to celebrate the night at a hotel on South Beach. Just then I realized I needed to change purses. Because we'd had a peaceful few weeks, my guard was down as I began to transfer items into my evening purse. My birth control pills fell out and David went out of control. I nodded as the fireworks that occurred in my house replayed.

Jodi laughed. "Yeah, I know I didn't want to come in."

The wind chime on the door jingled and interrupted my moment of reflection. We both sang, "Good morning, Dr. Freid."

A party hat rested on his bald top. His thin brown hair stuck out on the sides. We looked at each other and shook our heads. He hugged Jodi, then me. "Happy New Year, ladies."

He got settled in his office and came back out to chat. I leaned on the counter resting the swollen side of my face in my right hand. He asked, "What did you do last night?"

I shook my head. He turned to Jodi. "And you?"

She was young, rich, and white. She always had something *awesome* to share. Although I tried to fight it, I envied her. She rambled about her night. "My friends and I ate on South Beach."

I was supposed to be on the Beach last night. As disappointment dismantled my shield, my hand slipped down from my face. I folded my arms and imagined the life that Jodi lived.

Dr. Freid glared at me. I swiftly shielded my face again with my hand. He chuckled. "Well, Jodi, sounds like you brought the year in right."

I sat there wondering how some people got favor and others got shit. Dr. Freid looked at me and shook his head before going to his office. He often gave me that look. I knew what he wanted to say, but was thankful that he kept his comments to himself.

It startled me when he yelled to the front in a demanding tone: "Laila, I need to speak with you."

My heart sank. I hated when he called my name like that. It always made me feel like my job was in jeopardy. Jodi looked at me and shrugged her shoulders. I did the same and rolled my eyes. She shushed me. "It's probably nothing. Go ahead."

I slouched into his office. From the doorway, I spoke: "Yes?"

He was taking off his cheap suit jacket. "Come in and close the door."

His intense gaze frightened me. I closed the door and nervously sat down. "Yes?"

He pushed his glasses up on his protruding nose. He took a deep breath. Paused. Another deep breath. Another pause.

Each passing second made me more and more anxious. No. Please don't tell me that you don't need my help. My eyes begged him not to fire me. He said, "Laila, I don't know what to say."

My voiced trembled. "Please don't fire me."

He forced a smile. "I'm not trying to fire you, Laila."

I relaxed in my seat. "Whew!"

He shook his head. "You're the best employee I've ever had."

I sighed. "Oh, Dr. Freid!"

He didn't allow much time for me to gloat over his compliment. "Which brings me to my point." He sighed. "You've been here for almost two years and I sometimes feel as if you're my daughter. You and Jodi."

I raised my eyebrows and nodded. He wiped sweat from beneath his glasses, obviously contemplating his next comment. "I have never pried into your private life."

I nodded and rested my elbow on the side of the chair, while attempting to cover my face with my hand. I nibbled on my bottom lip. My eyes shifted around the room.

"I think I've stood by for long enough."

He took another deep breath. His eyes filled. "Laila, I know."

I didn't respond. A tear rolled down his face. He pulled his glasses off. Still, I was silent.

"You are so smart and so beautiful."

I looked down at the carpet. How could I look him in the eye?

"Laila, why?"

I often wish I knew how to explain my life, my situation. Trying to sound convincing, I said, "Dr. Freid, it's not what you think it is."

He stood up and sat on the desk in front of me. He put his hand out. Without looking at him, I put my hand in his. "Laila, I can help you."

I shook my head. "I'm fine. Honestly."

He put his hand on my bruised face. "You're not fine. I see your face like this at least once a week. I can't take it anymore."

He looked at me waiting for a response. I looked away. He continued to talk. "How can you let some man just do this to you?"

He huffed. "I've known what was going on with you since the day you walked in here." He grunted. "Twenty-year-old women don't get back injuries like that from falling down stairs."

In efforts to avoid eye contact, I looked up, down, left, right. His eyes chased mine. As he detailed how he knew, I felt like a failure. How had I been so careless? As if I could change my situation. He pleaded. "Why? How?"

His words hurt. Finally, I confessed. "I don't know what to do."

"Leave, Laila. Leave. You don't have to take it."

My balled fists covered my eyes, as I literally fought the tears that were trying to escape. I vigorously shook my head.

"You have to get out of this relationship."

He could never understand. He spoke as if it were so simple.

I huffed and looked him directly in the eye. I let the tears fall as I explained, "I don't have anywhere to go. I don't have any family."

He looked baffled. "You don't have anywhere you can go?"

I shook my head. "Nowhere that he won't find me. I've tried to leave before, but I don't know where to go."

He walked back around the desk and sat in his chair. Jodi knocked on the door. She spoke through the door, "Mr. Gregory is here for his 9:30 appointment."

I wiped my tears and blew my nose. Dr. Freid walked to the door. "Get yourself together. I'll prepare the room. Stay here."

He left me in the office to think. Thoughts about leaving filled my head. As always, love or fear, one or the other told me I needed to stay. David needed me. By the time Dr. Freid returned to his office, the desire to plan an exit strategy was a thought of the past. He asked. "Laila, are you okay?"

I nodded. He sat down. "You can tell me it's none of my business if you want."

"No, I don't feel like that."

He folded his hands. "How do you feel?"

I shrugged my shoulders.

"Laila, if you want help, I can help."

I twisted my lips. "I love him."

He said, "Unbelievable."

I looked into his eyes. "And he loves me too. He doesn't mean it. It's only when he drinks."

His blue eyes pierced through me. "Laila, he's going to kill you if you don't get out of there."

I curled my lips. "He won't kill me."

"As I said before, if you ever want help, I can help." He walked to the door. "You have makeup on your scrubs. Do you have another top here?"

I nodded. "Go ahead and change."

When I walked in the house, David was upstairs. I went into the kitchen to begin dinner. He'd already pulled a chicken breast from the freezer. I called up to him, "David, I'm home."

No answer. I continued preparing dinner. I heard him stumbling down the steps. He walked up behind me. "What's up?"

He pushed himself against my behind, obviously wanting me to acknowledge that he was aroused. I pretended I could feel his small nature through his jeans. I moaned, "Hey, baby."

He tossed his beer bottle in the trash. I kissed him. "You don't have any appointments today?"

"People ain't looking for houses after the holiday. It's gonna be slow for a minute. You know that."

I walked to the pantry to find a side dish. "What do you want with this chicken?"

He didn't respond. He had an inquisitive look on his face. I smiled. "What's wrong?"

"That ain't the same shirt you wore to work this morning."

Totally unprepared for the comment, I stuttered. "Um . . . I . . . um . . . I spilled some juice on my other shirt and I . . ."

"Laila, why you lying?"

"I'm not lying."

"Since when have you admitted to lying?"

"David, calm down. Remember, you said no fighting this year."

He stood in my face. "We're not fighting. I just want an answer."

I pleaded, "David, I gave you an answer. What more do you want?"

"Never mind. Fuck it."

I turned back to the sink and continued washing the chicken breast. He grabbed another beer and stormed away.

When I finished cooking, I went upstairs to shower. I purposely undressed in front of the television. He mumbled, "Come here."

I walked to the side of the bed. "What's up?"

He patted the empty space beside him, "Lay down."

I snuggled next him. He said, "I'm sorry for questioning you."

I accepted his apology with a long kiss. He climbed on me and began kissing my breasts. He slipped his hand down into my candy dish. He pushed one finger in at a time. He shoved deeper and deeper. "That's how you like it, right?"

I shook my head. "I like you in there."

"No you don't."

I moaned. "Um. Yes I do."

He pulled his boxers down. "You want this little thing?"

I nodded. He slipped inside. No friction. Painless indulgence. He asked his usual question, "You want a bigger one. Don't you?"

I shook my head. He pumped harder and harder. My head banged against the headboard. He ejaculated all over me. Jokingly, I wiped some on him.

He shouted, "Don't wipe that shit on me."

I giggled. "It's yours."

"I don't give a fuck."

I headed for the bathroom. He jumped in the shower with me. When we stepped out, he lifted me up on the sink. He entered me again. My joyful cloud rained puddles. Tension formed in his face with each stroke. He frowned, "Laila, you been with someone else?"

I shook my head. He accused. "I can feel it."

I whispered, "Shut up."

Suddenly he rammed my head into the mirror. Stunned, I screamed, "What's wrong with you?"

He stormed out of the bathroom. I followed, "David, I'm not fucking anybody else."

"Get away from me."

I grabbed his arm. "Why don't you trust me?"

He turned around and shoved my head into the wall. I pushed him back.

He wrapped his hand around my throat. Less than twenty-four hours into the New Year and the resolution was nullified. I sniffed my tears back and stared into his eyes. He threw jabs at my ribs, as if he wanted me to regurgitate my indiscretions.

In the midst of an episode, I couldn't imagine staying with him. Once it ended, I couldn't gather the strength to leave. My head tossed side to side. He grabbed a lamp and cracked it over my head. Debris cut my naked body. Light shot to my brain. My life flashed before my eyes. Dr. Freid's warning shouted in my ear. It echoed. *He's going to kill you. To kill you.* What did I have to live for?

As I broke bread with the man that was killing me slowly, it came to me. I had to live for me. I am all I have. If I stay here, I'll die.

CHAPTER 3

When Dr. Freid walked into the office, I anxiously followed him back into his office. I closed his door. My apprehension was gone. Loud and clear, I said. "Dr. Freid, I need your help. I don't know how I'm going to manage, but I want out."

He smiled. As if I were in a race, my chest heaved. I was running for my life. He ran his fingers through the thin swoop of hair that covered his bald spot. "Whatever you need . . ."

In a fighter's stance, I shrugged my shoulders and shook my head. "I don't know what I need. I just have to get out of there."

He smiled. "When did you come to that conclusion?"

"Yesterday . . ."

Baffled by my twenty-four hour change, he tilted his head. "After we talked."

I raised my shirt up and turned my back to him. "After this."

I caught a glimpse of the distress on his face before he covered it with his hand. He shook his head and closed his eyes tightly. He was the father of four girls, and my scars pained him more than they hurt me.

He breathed heavily. "Look, I'll get you a place."

Miami was no option. He would find me. I shook my head.

"Dr. Freid, I just need enough money to get out of town. If I can get out of here, I can get away."

He released a sympathetic sigh, "What do you plan to do in another town?"

How could I explain that I had a skill that would always pay the bills? Though I hated the thought of returning to that life, I would if I had to, but not in South Florida. "I don't know. But I can't stay here. He ain't gonna leave me alone if I stay here."

He crossed his fingers and tapped on the desk. "You have to have a better plan than that. Or you'll be back where you started."

"No I won't. I'm tired. I swear."

I scattered my heart all over his desk. "He promised me this year would be better. I believed him. I trusted him. I can't do it anymore."

"What happened the last time you tried to leave?"

At first I didn't speak. Then, I lowered my head, "A part of me wanted him to catch me."

He looked so disgusted, obviously I sounded foolish. He folded his arms, "Laila, what's going to make this time any different?"

"I never had anyone to help me."

He forced a smile. "You have me now."

I nodded. "Thank you."

He stood up. "Laila, do you have any idea on where you want to go?"

I thought about all of the dreams. The one ludicrous dream I had as a child of moving to New York and becoming a famous model. After being convinced that I looked like a monster, I stopped believing in dreams. So I shrugged my shoulders. "No, not really. I've never even been outside of South Florida."

"Don't worry. I'll take care of you."

By the time the office closed, Dr. Freid found me a job with an old college buddy in Philadelphia. How could I just go and live in a major city alone? What if I didn't like the doctor I'd be working for? What did I have to lose? I remember when I last danced at the night club, Gina told me, "You'll be back."

Believing that I found my guardian angel, I shook my head. "No, I won't."

She chuckled. "Once you're in this game, you always come back. The money is too good. You're like a drug addict. You're always recovering. When you're faced with rough times, you come back to what you know."

When I walked out of that club, I cut off contact with everyone. I didn't want the temptation. Being faced with entering a new city alone and broke, I thought about Gina's warning. If I had to return, at least it would be a different city.

When we closed the office, I stayed later to discuss the plans in privacy. Dr. Freid's friend offered me a position in Philadelphia. *Liberty*. He also had a temporary living arrangement for me. I planned to abandon my car, which was in David's name. We opened an online business bank account for Freid Chiropractics, which I would use as a direct deposit until I felt it was safe to use my own name. I sat there listening to Dr. Freid's arrangements. They were so well planned. The idea felt right. My time had finally arrived.

When I left work, I bought a huge roller duffle bag. I went to Wal-Mart to buy toiletries. I stocked up on everything I anticipated needing. I stuffed everything in the duffle bag and put it in my trunk.

When I got home, my heart pounded because I was one hour later than normal. I brought in bags from Wal-Mart to support my alibi. David was dancing around the kitchen when I walked in. I crept cautiously up to him. "Hey, baby."

He turned around and kissed my cheek. "I guess you stopped at Wal-Mart, huh?"

I nodded. "What are you cooking?"

"Steaks."

Relieved that I didn't have to cook, I sighed. "Thank you."

As I watched Dr. Jekyll float around the kitchen, I began

doubting my decision. When it was time to leave, could I really go?

I walked upstairs and stepped into the walk-in closet. I glanced at all the clothes I'd gathered over the years and I tried to figure out a way to get everything out. There was no obvious solution.

For the next ten days, I'd tuck one or two of my favorite garments into my workbag. I'd transfer the items to the duffle bag when I got to work. As the days went on, I was nervous that he'd notice empty hangers. Still, I continued as planned and my runaway bag was filled with my essentials.

David, on the other hand was trying hard to live up to his resolution, possibly just one-tenth of a second too late. As the time approached, I began to debate. What if he did change? Was it fair to leave without giving him the chance to say good-bye?

On the day of my departure, I left for work as usual. When I got to the front door, as if he feared my not returning, he tramped down the stairs. He startled me. My eyes blinked rapidly, as I clutched my workbag. He sang my name, "Laila."

I mumbled, "Yes."

He came over and softly pecked my cheek. "You didn't give me a kiss this morning."

I sighed. "I'm sorry, baby."

I searched for confirmation in his eyes. Afraid of what I might see, I grabbed the doorknob. He patted my shoulder, "Have a good one, baby."

I smiled. I forgave. When I heard the door close behind me, tears rolled down my face.

CHAPTER 4

When I pulled up to the office, Dr. Freid was sitting patiently in his car. I raised my finger, motioning for him to give me a moment. I opened the good-bye card that I contemplated giving David. Initially, I wrote: *I'm sorry*. Then, I scratched it out and wrote: *David, Thank you for everything, but I'm tired. Don't worry. I'm safe*.

On the left hand side of the card, I scribbled a poem that I wrote to him thanking him for saving me. Before I got out of the car, I kissed the envelope and left a lipstick print. As I pulled my bag from the trunk of the car, my heart beat rapidly. Could David actually be watching me? I looked around. No one. Nothing. There was no reason to stay. I absorbed it. I exhaled and tossed my bag into Dr. Freid's trunk.

Finally, I plopped in his Pontiac Le Sabre. He looked more confused than me. He stared at me and bunched his bushy eyebrows together. "You ready?"

I nervously nodded. "Yeah." I shrugged my shoulders. "I guess."

He dropped his head. Then, looked back at me. "Laila, I'm only doing this because I believe you deserve a chance. You're a nice girl. In fact, you're one of the best employees I've ever had."

He pinched my chin, "You're special. I hope you know that."

"Dr. Freid, no one has ever done something so nice for me in my life. I really appreciate everything."

He put his hand on top of mine. "Don't disappoint me."

"Oh, Dr. Freid, I won't disappoint you."

"I don't want to hear about you coming back to be with that loser."

I nodded. He demanded. "Laila, I mean it."

I nodded. "Okay."

Trying to quickly escape the lecture, I asked, "Do you really think it's a good idea to leave the car here?"

He nodded and chuckled. "That's what we discussed, right?"

"Yeah, but when he realizes I'm gone, he's going to go crazy and I just don't want anything to happen to you."

The thought upset me. He rubbed my leg to calm me. "I'm not worried Laila. I'm not afraid of him. Just as planned, I'll call him around five this evening and tell him you never came into work."

I still felt scared to actually execute this crazy plan, but I nodded. He continued, "By that time, you'll be in Philly, getting settled."

He paused. "You left a note in the car, right?"

I nodded. He nodded. He put his hand on top of mine. "Don't worry about me. I'm the last person he'll think about."

I raised my eyebrow. We both laughed. He clarified. "He'll never think you'd be in Philadelphia. Trust me. I can handle this."

I sighed. "Okay. Should we get moving?"

Before we pulled off, he handed me a big lump of cash in a Bank of America envelope. "Here, this should hold you over while you get on your feet."

I pushed his hand away. "Dr. Freid, you've done enough. I have some cash."

"Take the money!" he said.

He stuffed it in the side pocket of my purse. I hugged his neck. "Thank you so much."

We took off for Fort Lauderdale airport. As we sat in rush hour traffic on 95 South, I thought about everything. I wanted to turn around, but when I looked at Dr. Freid I heard his request, *Don't disappoint me.* After all he'd done, how could I? We pressed on.

When signs for the airport began to pop up, I felt sick. Like a slave afraid of freedom, I sat up in my seat. Three miles. One and a quarter mile. The distance to the airport decreased. The distance to Coconut Creek increased. It was no longer my home. The planes flying overhead frightened me more.

My first time flying and I was going to be alone. I looked at Dr. Freid. "Are you going to come in with me?"

He nodded. "I'll come in and get you situated, but I can't go to the gate with you."

I pouted. "Why?"

He rubbed my leg. "Only ticketed passengers can go through the security check point."

As if I knew what he was talking about, I nodded.

We parked in daily parking and he carried my luggage over to the terminal. He handed me my ticket and instructed me as we stood at the self check-in kiosk. Paranoia had me searching the airport for a sight of David. He pointed to the ticket. "See, you're in Section B." He explained the boarding procedure of Southwest Airlines. I nodded, trying to understand to the best of my ability. He explained that when I got to Philly to follow baggage claim signs. I took a deep breath and we went down the escalator to the security check-in. He pointed, "Your gate is right through there."

My breathing got heavier. Louder. We hugged. "You'll be fine. Dr. Ryder's going to meet you at the airport. He has your number and you have his. Right?"

I nodded. As we stood in front of the security attendant requesting my boarding pass and ID, he hugged me again. When I handed the attendant my rights of passage, he stepped back. He nodded proudly as I traveled through the roped out maze. I waved as I began going through the metal detector. "Ma'am, is this your stuff?"

I nodded. "Push it up on the belt."

I pushed my small backpack and headed through the detector. "Is this your purse?"

I nodded. "Make sure all your belongings are on the belt before stepping forth."

I put my boarding pass on the belt. "Keep your pass in your hands."

I wanted to scream. Too many damn instructions. Couldn't they see that I was bewildered? Damn. Finally, I stepped through the metal detector. Beep. Beep. They sent me back through. Beep. Beep.

"Ma'am, empty your pockets."

I did so. I looked back at Dr. Freid. My face cried for help, but he smiled. They instructed. "Take your shoes off. Put them on the belt."

Finally, I was cleared. I waved at Dr. Freid and he waved back. I gestured. "I'll call you."

I stopped at the newsstand in the terminal and grabbed some snacks for my journey. Also, I got my favorite sleeping drug, NyQuil.

After what felt like hours, I was on the plane, seated and prepared for takeoff. My stomach plummeted. My eyes watered. I curled up to the window. As the plane slowly drifted back from the gate, I panicked. My hands pressed against the window. Where the hell did I think I was going? Speed increased. The plane tilted toward the sky. My heart rolled into my throat. As it rose higher, my emotions sank lower. My head pounded. I sat there. I prayed. I played in my hair. I clicked my nails. Finally, I resorted to my nighttime cocktail. I took a shot of NyQuil to sedate myself. Within seconds my eyelids felt like five-pound weights.

David had stormed through the house screaming, "Laila!"

I lay in the bed, afraid to answer. The sound of his footsteps got louder. "Laila!"

He walked into the bedroom, "What the hell you doing calling Dr. Freid all hours of the damn night?"

Startled by his accusations, I stuttered, "I don't know whatchu talking about."

I scooted away from him. He shoved my cell phone bill in my face. "You fucking that white motherfucka."

He mashed my face with the palm of his hand. "You quittin' that job tomorrow."

I pleaded. "I'm not sleeping with him." I walked away and mumbled. "And I'm not quitting my job either."

He yanked my hair. My neck snapped back. "You gonna quit if I tell you to quit."

Willing to accept my punishment, I shook my head in an attempt to get away and to warn him that I had no intentions to quit. My resistance startled him. He frowned. "Don't fucking play with me, girl."

I softly chuckled. He wrestled me to the bed. I smirked at him. His punches no longer caused me pain. I didn't struggle. I lay there for the usual routine as he straddled me. The affect of my nonchalance was evident in his bitter mug. He struck me across my face with his back hand. My head snapped to the opposite side. I didn't beg for his sympathy. He smacked me again.

I refused to grant him the reaction he awaited. With each smack, he yelled. "Bitch!"

My head flicked from side to side. Someone tapped me. I jumped. My fist balled. I looked around. The flight attendant smiled. "I need you to bring your seat back up to an upright position to prepare for landing."

As the plane descended, my anxiety increased. I looked down at the buildings. I was in new territory. Would I regret this choice? Just as the plane touched down, my heart splashed into my gut. I looked at the lady sitting next to me. She smiled. I took deep breaths.

People rushed from the plane when it stopped, but I was hesitant. Had I really gotten away? No way had two hours passed. I pulled myself up on the seat in front of me and looked around the plane. What if he followed me?

As I walked to baggage claim, I felt nauseated. People hustled around me. I called Dr. Ryder while standing at the belt awaiting my bag. He answered. "Hello."

"Hi, this is Laila."

"Yes, Laila. I'm outside. I'm actually heading into baggage claim."

The heartbeat raging in my chest settled a bit. I noticed my bag and grabbed it from the belt. "Great. I'll stay here." I chuckled. "I'm wearing the blue and white scrubs."

The cold air crept in when the sliding glass doors opened. I quickly rummaged through my duffle bag for the new bomber jacket I'd bought. As I bit the tags off, Dr. Ryder walked up to me, "Laila."

Damn. Dr. Ryder slightly stole my breath. I gasped for air. Without a second thought, I hugged him. He leaned down and wrapped his broad arms around me. He had thick, dark brown hair. His complexion was tanned and smooth. Not quite what I'd expect of a friend of Dr. Freid.

Finally, while slipping on my new coat, I said, "Hello, Dr. Ryder."

"Call me Daniel outside of the office."

Wow! Our relationship was off to a quick start. I smiled. A little uncomfortable with saying his first name, I mumbled, "Um, I'm really glad you were able to help me out."

"Oh no. I was in desperate need of another assistant. Do you know how hard it is to find a good one?"

I shook my head. "Michael always had good things to say about you. Hell, when he said you needed a change, I made an offer." He sighed. "Do you have any more luggage?"

Partially embarrassed, I said, "No." I shook the strap of the duffle bag. "Just this."

"You packed everything up in that bag?"

I smiled. My limited belongings obviously required some explanation. "I need a new start. I left everything but the must haves behind."

Uncertain as to how much Dr. Freid shared with him, I decided to leave it at that. I had no plans to spray paint my story all over Philly.

He appeared satisfied and didn't pry any further. He shrugged his shoulders. "Well, I guess I know how you feel."

He slung the bag over his shoulder and we walked out of the airport into the freezing cold. My legs transformed in to icicles in my thin pants. An additional set of footsteps tapped behind us. I tucked my chin in my jacket, but continuously peeped over my shoulder. No one followed. Was the sound in my head? He laughed, "Laila, are you expecting someone?"

In a jittery tone, I said, "No, why do you say that?"

He shook his head. "Never mind."

We got into the car. He gave me a brief overview of the community I'd be living in.

"The building is so-so, but the price is nice for the community."

I shrugged my shoulders, "Well, I didn't really expect to be living in the lap of luxury."

He laughed, but I was honest. I was no stranger to living in subpar housing.

"It's about three blocks from the office."

I raised my eyebrows. "Wow, I expected to be catching the bus for awhile."

He patted my knee. "Nope. We got you all squared away. A nice place, close to work." He smiled. "I like to make my employees happy. Michael will handle your first three months' rent." He chuckled. Oblivious to my frustration, he continued, "After that, half of your rent will come directly out of your check. I signed the lease as a business rental."

I covered my mouth, "Oh, no."

"What's wrong?"

I shook my head, "He's done enough."

"Laila, don't . . ."

I huffed. "But . . ."

"Don't worry. He has money to throw away."

I put my elbow on the door and propped my chin up. I shook my head. "How much is the rent?"

"The landlord is a good friend of mine. He's giving you a furnished studio for $600 a month."

Why were these people being so nice? It was as if I was in the midst of a dream. As I recalled, I felt the same when I moved in with David. He continued to give me the specifics of where I'd be living.

"You're in apartment 4G. I think. It's on the key. Anyway, you have a television, stereo, VCR." He chuckled. "You'll have to buy your own DVD."

I smiled. He finished the rundown of my amenities. Finally, he asked if I wanted to get some groceries. I nodded anxiously. "Yes, definitely."

He took me to Pathmark. I picked up the essential items. *Sugar Smacks. Peanut Butter. Jelly. Strawberry Frosted Pop Tarts. Milk. Doritos. Salt and Vinegar Chips.* I bought some paper plates and utensils. We rode through a quiet residential neighborhood. He pointed. "This is Spruce Street. The office is right on Spruce and Tenth."

We drove a few blocks past the office. "You're right up here on Spruce, between Thirteenth and Fourteenth."

The building looked as if they had dropped a high-rise project building right in the middle of the set of the Cosby Show. Unconsciously, I frowned. "Here?"

He repeated his disclaimer, "It's not the greatest, but this is Center City. You're in the middle of everything."

I nodded. My heart beat rapidly. I took a deep breath.

He drove past the building and gave me a mini tour. "Up here on Sixteenth, you'll find all the stores you need." We circled around onto another one-way street. Then, he made another right. "This is Market Street. There are a lot of shops here as well. The Gallery is right there. That's an indoor mall. This is Tenth Street. If you go straight up here, you'll run back into the office."

As if I'd remember any of it in ten minutes, I nodded. We drove back up to the pitiful looking building. I smiled nervously.

He clicked his hazard lights on and hopped out. I slowly opened the door. I slouched into the building. When we got to the narrow elevator, he said, "Laila, I'm going to let you get settled." He pulled the roller handle from my big bag. He pushed the handle towards me. As if I didn't already feel stupid, he joked. "I see you don't need much help with your bags."

I smiled. "Please do come in."

He joked. "Nah, I don't want to cramp your style."

Shocked at his correct usage of slang, I covered my mouth and giggled.

"Honestly, I really have to head home. My wife is expecting me."

My face drooped. I wanted to beg him. What if someone was hiding in my closet? I looked out of the window; the sun had gone down. I was scared. Oblivious to my desperation, he continued. "I'm not expecting you at work until Tuesday. So you have five days to lay back and relax. Explore the city. If you need anything, give me a call. Otherwise, I'll see you Tuesday at nine."

I pressed the up arrow.

He said, "Hey, I almost forgot. Hold up a minute."

He ran back to the car. He came back carrying a bunch of magazines. "These should help you get around the city." He opened one of the magazines. "There's a map of Center City in here. There's also a transit map."

I nodded. "Thanks."

He walked back to the door. "See you Tuesday. Don't hesitate to call if you need anything."

I stood in the door of the rickety elevator. How could he just leave me standing there alone? With nowhere to go, but up, I pressed four. When I got off, I looked left, then right. I went right, then left. Finally I stood in front of 4G. I turned the key. My heart thumped. I pushed softly. The door screeched. I whispered, "Hello."

No one answered. I tiptoed into the petite place. No hiding places, just open space. There was a small couch opposite the door. A naked double bed sat in the middle of the floor. Oh no! I had no sheets, no blankets. What was I thinking?

I looked to the right. Every rack in the miniature bathroom was bare. I contemplated calling Dr. Ryder back, but I decided against it. I sat on the mattress, folded my arms and looked out of the window. Did I make the right decision? Still bundled in my coat, I rocked back and forth. I wanted to go home. Then, I wanted stay. Afraid to go home, more afraid to stay. I pulled a bag of Doritos from my backpack and began nibbling. Trying to silence the confusion in my head, I turned on the television. I took my coat off, balled it up and made a pillow. I curled up on the bed, hugged my Doritos, and drifted into a light nap. Noises in the hall shook me. I gazed into the sky for hours. Finally, I resorted to more NyQuil.

The sun beaming through the sheer curtains woke me. Relieved that I made it through the night, I dialed the office, and disguised my voice. "Yes, I'd like to speak with Dr. Freid."

Jodi paused, "The doctor's with a patient. Can I help you?"

"I'll call back later."

She paused again. "Okay."

Within minutes, my cell phone rang. I jumped. I was careful not to touch it. I was afraid of the possibilities on the other end. Dr. Freid. Jodi. David.

I let it stop. Then, I dialed the office back.

"Dr. Freid here . . ."

Whew! I whispered, "Dr. Freid?"

He spoke loudly, "Yes, Ms. Walker."

"Did he come there?" I asked.

"Sure, you can come in this morning."

I heard his office door close. His voice was a soft whisper. "I called your house around six yesterday and told him that you never came in. Jodi supported my story, though I believe she may be a little suspicious."

I could give a hoot about Jodi. Anxious to hear more about David's reaction, I asked, "What did he say?"

He said. "I told him the car was here, but we hadn't seen you. I pretended to be concerned. I asked if he knew where you might be.

"He was at the office before I could blink. He went straight to the car. He walked in with the card in his hand and cried in my arms."

Shocked that he didn't go off, I asked, "Are you serious? He didn't accuse you of anything?"

"Nope. He let me read the card and begged me to let him know if I ever hear from you."

Adrenaline pumped through my veins. I was free. Dr. Freid was safe. We did it! In the midst of my excitement, I felt horrible. "What did he say while he was crying?"

"He admitted he needed help. He said . . ." He paused. "Never mind."

"What, Dr. Freid?"

He cleared his throat. "He claims he wants help."

My heart dropped. Feeling like I'd betrayed my only friend, I wanted to cry. Just as I was about to beat myself up with regret, Dr. Freid warned. "Most men like that never change."

I nodded and sighed. "You're right."

"He knows you're okay. Don't worry about him. Okay?"

I nodded.

"I told him if I ever hear from you, I would tell you to call."

I sighed. "Okay."

"Laila, it's going to be all right. Don't worry. He's not going to find you."

I sniffed. "I hope not."

"So, how are your accommodations?"

"Everything is wonderful. I'm going out today to buy everything I need. I don't have anything."

"Get whatever you need. That credit card has a ten thousand dollar limit."

"You really can't imagine how much I appreciate this. I promise, I'll find a way to pay you back."

He cleared his throat. "Don't worry about that. Just be safe and get used to your new home. Call me when you can."

In the same scrubs I'd had on for twenty-four hours, I wandered out into the city. My first stop was the Gap. I picked up a few pair of jeans and some sweaters. Then, I went to Vicky's to buy my favorite cotton panties and bras. Despite not having to pay the credit card bill, I still shopped sensibly. I didn't know how long I'd need to use it.

I bought linens, towels, utensils. I trotted around freely and found myself smiling for no reason. Each time I realized that I was having fun, I would get consumed with guilt. My emotions flip-flopped. Happy to be free, but plagued by what I'd done.

After a long day, I strolled back to the projects looking like a bag lady. My cell phone didn't ring. There was no one to watch my every move. I shopped freely, aimlessly, and I didn't give a damn about what time I got home.

I took my sheets to the laundry room. While I waited, I snacked on Sour Patch Kids and Salt and Vinegar Chips. I patted my feet as I began to feel the sugar rush. My mouth puckered from the sour taste. I smiled. I could eat candy all evening without anyone worrying me about dinner.

When my linens were fresh and clean, I fluffed them on the bed. I flopped down and entangled myself in the sheets. I kicked wildly. My entire body stretched across the bed. I escaped. Oh my God! I did it. Unspeakable joy came over me. No way could I ever turn around.

Wrapped in my homemade toga, I paced through the room. I stopped at the bathroom. I pulled my ponytail holder off. I ran my fingers through my hair. David's voice demanding that I not cut my hair filtered through my brain and made me want to do it even more. I pulled it behind my ears. It would validate my freedom.

CHAPTER 5

I spent two entire days talking myself into cutting my hair. After passing the Hair Cuttery three times, I finally went in. The huge "Walk-ins Welcomed" sign invited me. When I walked inside, the hair scattered around the floor reminded me of when I involuntarily got my hair cut, which happened to be the last time that I had anything other than my ends clipped. I was thirteen and being transferred to my ninth residence, but into my first group home. I'll never forget how my heart pounded when I stepped up to that door. Loud voices escaped the house. I looked at my social worker. He patted my shoulder, "Don't worry. You'll love it here."

The staff member on duty opened and we walked in. Eight girls sat in the living room. They looked at me, but no one spoke. The young lady took us on a tour. She then escorted me into the boxing ring, introduced me and left me standing there. One of the girls, joking, asked, "You got Indian in your family . . ?"

Another asked. "Are you Dominican?"

"Are you Haitian?"

Most kids were products of the foster care system because their parents or someone in their family abused them. Others were there because their parents simply neglected them or were incarcerated. Then, there was the rare few of us that were rejected before birth. Our papers stated, mother unknown, father unknown. No connection to our heritage.

I said, "I don't know."

The "before fight" rumble began to percolate in my belly as they stared at me as if I was an alien. One of the older girls laughed, "As black as your ass is, you know she ain't nothing but black."

Another girl stood up and pulled my ponytail, which hung a few inches above my waist. "This shit ain't real."

Defending the one thing that people thought was beautiful about me, I yanked away. "It is mine."

I rushed into the hall where my social worker stood, my eyes begged him. Before I could speak, he said, "Laila, you'll be fine. I'll come see you later this week."

He walked out. The lady rapidly transformed into a witch, "Get your ass in there with everybody else!"

I slouched into the room. They teased. I responded with snide remarks. When the witch showed me where I'd be sleeping, I lay in the bed, fully dressed. I planned to get out of that place as soon as possible. Later that night, a buzzing sound woke me. A group of girls hovered over me. A few of them pinned me down. Others cut my hair with scissors. And the one I'll never forget raked my head with the clippers. I struggled to get away. I yelled for help, as chunks of my hair fell to the floor. They laughed. They hit fives. They left me there, lying in a bed of hair. I wept all night.

My social worker moved me the next day. Imagine being thirteen with a bald head walking into a new group home.

The receptionist interrupted me. "Can I help you?"

I blinked out of my daze, "Um . . . are you accepting walk-ins today?"

She looked up at me and smacked her lips. "We accept walk-ins *every day*."

"Can I get my hair cut?"

She said, "Have a seat and the first available stylist will come and get you."

A slim girl, who looked no older than twelve walked over and asked me to sit in her chair. I followed her. I lifted my hair out of my coat and peeled it off. I shook my hair down.

She smiled. "I'm Aisha."

"And I'm Laila."

She ran her fingers through my hair. "Laila, your hair is so pretty."

"Thanks."

"How you want it?"

I pulled the picture of Halle Berry on the cover of *Essence* from my purse, "Like this."

She walked around to face me. "You want to cut all this hair?"

I nodded. "You must be crazy. I wish my hair would grow this long."

I folded my arms. "It's too hard to maintain."

She shook her head. "Okay. I'm here to serve you."

I nodded. "I want some color, too. Maybe some light brown highlights."

She held my chin in her hand, slightly mugged and nodded. "I think cranberry highlights would be fly on you."

I shrugged my shoulders. "Okay. Let's do cranberry."

She chuckled. "Are you sure?"

I nodded.

"I'm going to cut it some before I lift the color."

She put a smock on me and pulled my hair up with a rubber band into one ponytail. She loosely braided the hair and put another rubber band on the end. She cut the ponytail off. My head felt ten pounds lighter. She dangled the long plait in front of me. "Here you go."

I laid it on my lap. I stroked it like a baby. So much hair . . . so many years . . . so many memories, I couldn't believe what I'd just done. I sighed. A new beginning.

She dyed and styled my hair in a relatively short time. She

pulled the clippers from her smock to add the finishing touches. That noise. That buzzing. It still sent chills up my spine. I cringed and covered my eyes. When she was done, she twirled the chair around to face the mirror. "It looks so good."

I slowly slid my hands from my face. A brand new woman stared at me.

Aisha appeared shocked at her own abilities, "You look so good."

I smiled. "Thanks."

She continued. "It becomes you so well."

As I was shaking hair from my clothes, I noticed other customers smiling and nodding. My skepticism subsided. I paid her and added a $10 tip. She smiled, "Girl, work that hairdo."

Her continuous compliments made me uneasy. I rushed out of the salon. The wind blew through my short hair. The cold air made me shiver. I stuffed my hands in my pocket and jogged to my building.

Once alone, I stood in the bathroom mirror for hours and adapted to the new me. My slim face thanked me, the unveiling of a hidden jewel. I smiled. I covered my mouth. I ran my fingers through my hair. I paced back and forth.

Eventually, I calmed down and grabbed my poetry notebooks from my bag. I flipped through one of the books. Years and years of poetry reeked of an abused woman . . . a neglected child saturated the pages. I scribbled the word *yesterday*, on the outside of the notebook. I browsed through the other one. There, I found poems of hope. I added another one. *Manifestation*.

CHAPTER 6

Iwalked three short blocks to my new place of employment. When I opened the doors to Ryder Chiropractic, my heart plunged as if I'd just performed an unfaithful act. A middle aged white lady with a smoker's voice said, "Are you Laila?"

I nodded. She introduced herself. "Hi. I'm Ann. Come on back."

I walked behind the desk. She pointed, "Hang your coat over there."

She proceeded to give me a tour of the relatively large office. "We're short staffed, but we manage."

She blew air and her fluffy bangs flew up. "Let's just say we're glad we have more help."

She pointed to an office. "This is Jordan's, I mean Dr. Maxwell's office."

Realizing the question in my eyes, she responded. "He's our intern. He only works two days a week."

I nodded. "This is where we do the X-rays. And, this is our physical therapy unit."

"This is really nice."

"Yeah. Dr. Ryder has put a lot into this office. The old office wasn't half as luxurious."

I nodded.

"We've only been in this office three years. The demand increased so we needed to upgrade."

She hit my shoulder and chuckled. Her laugh gave me the creeps. "You know how that is."

She coughed and instructed me to follow her to the front. "Dr. Ryder wants me to get you acquainted with how things work around here. He'll be in around twelve."

I shrugged my shoulders. "Okay."

"Tuesdays and Thursdays we're open from twelve to six. And Monday, Wednesdays and Fridays, we're open from nine to three."

I folded my arms and listened to her systematic daily schedule. "Dr. Maxwell works on Tuesday and Thursday. There were two assistants until two weeks ago. Now, there's you and another lady, Beth. She comes in when she feels like it. That's like two times a week."

She laughed. "Honestly, though, she rarely comes in. Someone is always sick in her house."

I smiled. "Wow. I guess it's cool if Dr. Ryder doesn't mind."

She shook her head. "Oh, he minds. Trust me. That's why you're here."

I shrugged my shoulders. "I guess."

By eleven thirty, Ann had literally told me all the office gossip and everything else I needed to know. She rambled like a CD on repeat. At some point, you get tired of hearing it. By the time Dr. Ryder walked in, I wanted her to shut up. She shook my arm. "Laila, here's Dr. Ryder."

I stood to shake his hand. He hugged me. "You look so different."

I ran my fingers through my hair. "My hair's different."

He studied my hairstyle. "Wow. It looks great on you. Did you color it?"

I nodded.

"It makes you look more mature. You look slimmer, too."

I frowned. "Slimmer?"

Can I get any slimmer? As he undressed me with his eyes, he apologetically said, "Oh no! You look great."

With my future in his hands, I ignored the discomfort and smiled. I bit the corner of my bottom lip and looked at the floor. I peeped up at him. "Thanks."

"I'm sure Ann has told you everything."

I smiled and nodded.

"Why don't you just hang out with her for the remainder of the day?"

I would rather run around the office naked before I listened to another one of her long stories. I pleaded, "Oh, she's shown me all around. I'm sure I can start setting up rooms today."

"I don't want to rush you."

"I'm sure that I want to start today."

He agreed. Then, in walks this 6-foot-2-inch muscular guy with dreadlocks pulled into a ponytail. His skin color was on the complete opposite side of the spectrum from mine, but his smile illuminated the office. Not at all what I typically consider attractive, but his sheer presence was magnetic.

Ann greeted him with a big hug. "Hi, Dr. Maxwell."

He reached his hand out to shake mine. Our eyes met. Mine quickly shifted to focus on Ann's computer screen.

His deep voice vibrated throughout my body. "Hi. I'm Jordan. Jordan Maxwell."

I nodded.

He chuckled. "And you are?"

"I'm sorry. My name is Laila."

"Laila." His charming smile made my stomach flutter.

I nodded.

"You have a beautiful name."

"Thanks."

He was carrying a Burger King bag. "I wish I'd known you were starting today. I would've brought you some lunch."

He pulled a burger and some fries out and put them on Ann's desk. He grabbed a few fries, stuffed them in his mouth. "See, they don't tell me anything around here."

I blushed. "That's okay."

"You can have some of my food if you want."

Though my stomach was growling like a grizzly bear, I declined. "No thanks. I'm okay."

"What time did you get here?"

Ann butted in, "Nine."

He looked surprised. "I know you're hungry."

I shook my head. "I'm okay."

He smirked. "Laila, you ain't gotta lie to me. I know Ann. She'll talk you to death and never ask if you need a cracker."

I tucked my lips in to restrain the laughter. Ann cracked up. "Jordan, stop." She cleared her throat. "Laila, you're welcome to break for lunch."

Jordan offered to go with me. Despite my refusal, he tagged along. The second we exited the office, his questions started.

"You from around here?"

I shook my head.

"Where you from, then?"

"Miami."

"How long you been here?"

"A week."

"How you meet Dr. Ryder?"

"I used to work for his friend in Miami."

As if it just hit him, he frowned. "What brought you to Philly from Miami?" He joked and sang the Will Smith song. "Welcome to Miami. Miami."

Though I was extremely attracted to Jordan, his questions were irritating me. I sighed. "I needed a change."

He smiled. "I can feel that."

Finally, inside McDonald's, his interrogation stopped momentarily. "Yeah, I'm from around here. Born and raised. I went to Lincoln. Then, I went away to chiropractic school in Missouri. Man, I couldn't wait to get back here."

Uncertain of what to say to keep his pressure off me, I nodded. On the walk back to the office, he started again.

"Any kids?"

I shook my head.

"Husband? Boyfriend?"

Suddenly thoughts of David filled my head. Before I could think about my response, I said, "Not anymore."

He laughed. "I know how that is. Did you leave him back in Miami?"

I nodded. When we walked back into the office, I was elated to see Ann. She talked too much to ask questions. Jordan walked into his office. I sat down beside Ann. She gave me a suspicious smirk. "Jordan's hot."

I smiled. "He's not bad."

"Not bad." She nodded slyly. "All the female patients request him when he's here. They say he has gifted hands."

I curled my lips. "You're funny."

She scooted forward in her chair. "Ask him to give you an adjustment. I bet you'll think the same thing."

I laughed. "Okay. I'll let you know."

When the patients started rolling in, I was running around like a kitten chasing a string. How did he ever manage with a part-time assistant? I ran from room to room, from Dr. Ryder's office to Dr. Maxwell's office. How many patients can one office accept per day?

By six o'clock, I was literally sweating. Dr. Ryder looked at me. "I hope you're not ready to quit."

I shook my head. "No, I'm not ready to quit."

He patted my shoulders. "I guess you see now why I was so anxious to get you here."

I smiled. "Thanks again."

He looked into my eyes. "No, thank *you*."

He offered to take me to dinner. I decided to pick up fast food and eat in the privacy of my little pad.

I grabbed my coat from the rack. Jordan came behind me. His

presence made me nervous. I fumbled with my coat. He grabbed it and gently helped me into it.

I mumbled, "Thanks." I smiled. "See you tomorrow."

With his arms folded, he smirked. "I don't work on Wednesdays."

"Oh, I forgot. I'll see you on Thursday."

He didn't respond. When I got to the door, he said, "Hold up. I'll walk with you."

Shit! He rushed in the back, got his things and came running. When we got outside, the cold air smacked me in the face. "Whew."

He looked at me. "You cold?"

I nodded. He laughed. "Why don't you talk?"

I shrugged my shoulders. Didn't he talk enough for the both of us? He sighed. "It's like pulling teeth to get you to say two words."

I smiled. "It's not that bad. I'm just quiet."

He laughed. "I see."

So, I wouldn't seem too suspicious, I offered an explanation. "I just don't know you well enough yet."

He opened his arms, "Don't I look trustworthy?"

Trust? Hell no! I don't trust anyone. Instead of revealing my true feelings, I nodded.

When we reached my building, I stopped. "Let me guess. You stay here."

"Um-huh."

"Dr. Ryder got the hookup. I used to stay here."

"He knows the landlord. Right?"

He nodded. "His peeps own this building and the building that I stay in."

"Where do you stay?"

"A few blocks away."

I pulled the door to the building. Jordan blocked it. "Have you had a Philly cheese steak yet?"

"No."

He gently pulled my arm. "Let's go then."

His aggression disturbed me. I lied, "I left some chicken out this morning." I stumbled over my words. "I have to um . . . I need to . . ."

He smiled. "You need to relax and come have a bite to eat with a coworker."

I took a deep breath. After a second or so without a viable excuse, I laughed. "Okay."

We walked to his place and drove his car to South Street. We went into a little hole in the wall, Jim's Steaks. The spot was all of ten feet wide, but the line wrapped around three times. I looked at Jordan. "I guess the steaks are good here."

He nodded. "The best."

He ordered and looked at me. I shrugged my shoulders. He laughed. "Make that two."

The cook slapped Cheese Whiz on my bread. I frowned. "I don't like that kind of . . ."

He cut me off. "Just try it. If you don't like it, I'll take you somewhere else."

When we got to the register, I pulled money out. He rolled his eyes at me. "Laila, I'm a gentleman."

"I just don't feel comfortable with you paying for dinner."

"Okay. You can take care of dinner on Thursday."

Did I tell him I would go to dinner with him again? We sat at the counter to eat our greasy sandwiches. He walked away to get condiments. I took a bite. It practically melted in my mouth. The scrumptious taste caused a pleasurable smile to surface.

Jordan nodded. "You like?"

I wiped my mouth. "Yes."

Jordan pretty much devoured his sandwich in five minutes. When he finished, he sat quietly and studied my every bite. Feeling as if I was the center of attraction, I pretended I was full and wrapped up my food.

On the ride back, I fiddled with my bag. He calmly asked, "Whatchu scared of?"

"Huh?"

He smiled at me. "You just seem scared."

I mumbled. "I'm not scared."

We were both silent for the rest of the ride. When we pulled up to my building, I thanked him.

"See you Thursday."

When I got out the car, I finally exhaled.

CHAPTER 7

I strolled home from work, feeling lonely. The notion of new-found freedom began to fade. I longed for David's voice, his touch. What was I thinking to pack up and leave my only friend? I looked at my cell phone. I pressed *nine*. What was I to say? I pressed *end*. It's not as if I could say I needed a break for a few days. He would kill me. In all my attempts to escape, I always found my way back like a lost puppy within twenty-four hours. I stuffed my phone back into my purse. I'd been gone much too long to run back home.

Hoping a fudge sundae would suppress the feelings of regret, I went into McDonald's to grab some food. I dined in. With my head hung low, I dipped my fries into my sundae. Slowly, I licked the ice cream from the fries. How I crave that salt and sugar contrast! As I made love to my food, my orgasm was interrupted. "Laila."

Jordan scooted onto the bench across from me. My eyes flickered. "Hello."

He slouched down. His long eyelashes reached out and held me. I blushed.

He tapped his fist on the table. "So how was your second day?"

I shrugged my shoulders. "Okay, I guess."

He reached over and grabbed a few fries. "You miss me?"

I raised my eyebrows. "Huh?"

He smiled. "I'm just messin' with you. Why you so serious?"

I rolled my eyes. "I'm not that serious."

"You're not that open either."

I took a deep breath and wondered how long it would be before I could trust him. "I have a fun side, too."

He leaned back and folded his arms. "That's a good thing, 'cause I feel it's my duty to show you around town. And I don't want you all stuffy while I'm trying to show you a good time."

I laughed. "You're a trip."

He pointed, "Oh, she smiles."

I twisted my lips. "Leave me alone."

He shook his head. "I'm not going to leave you alone." He stood up while I gathered up my trash. He pinched my cheek. "Not until I find the real Laila."

Chills rippled throughout my body. *Gifted hands.* I shivered. I staggered. He grabbed the tray. "You all right?"

I nodded. "Yeah, I'm okay."

When we got outside, he grabbed my backpack from my shoulder. I yanked it back.

With his arms raised high, he relented. "I'm sorry, sweetheart. I was just trying to be a gentleman."

I had to laugh at my own reservation. "I'm just protective of my things."

"You act like you're hiding something."

Shocked by his presumption, I stopped and huffed. "Why I gotta be hiding something?"

He shook his dreads out. "It's just the feeling I get. It's cool though."

When we arrived at my building, I asked, "Were you following me?"

He propped one arm up on the other, cupped his chin in his hand, and leaned back. "Actually, no. I went into the office to pick up something from Dr. Ryder. When I passed McDonald's, I saw a beautiful girl eating alone. I decided to join her."

I bashfully thanked him. And without a second thought, asked if he wanted to come in.

He declined. "I'm studying for my boards. I gotta get home and hit the books."

He stood in front of me. The distance between us so narrow, his breathing hypnotized me. I felt dazed. My lips unconsciously parted. My eyelids slightly lowered. My clitoris pulsated.

He put his hand out and shook mine. "All right, Laila, I'll catch you tomorrow."

The slightest gust of wind could have knocked me over. I nodded and stumbled over my words. "Yeah . . . um . . . yeah. Catch you tomorrow."

I turned around and tripped. I laughed. Jordan tried not to. "You all right?"

Too embarrassed for more reasons than one to face him, I nodded and rushed into the building.

Jordan's face accompanied me through the night. His smile adorned my sweet dreams. Noon could not come fast enough. When Jordan walked in the office, butterflies lined my stomach. When I looked up at him, he turned to me.

He tapped the top of my head, "What's up, Laila?"

Ann looked at me. She blushed. When Jordan walked in the back, she said, "You should get an adjustment today."

I shooed her. "I haven't even gotten my X-rays yet."

"Beth can do them for you." She yelled for Beth. "Can you do an X-ray for Laila?"

Jordan walked out before Beth. "You haven't gotten an X-ray yet?" As if he'd be honored, he said, "I can do it."

Oh no! I looked at Ann. She smiled. "That's right, Jordan. You can do it."

She added. "You have close to thirty minutes before any patients come in."

I looked at Ann. Mischievously smiling, she waved her hand. "Go ahead."

Jordan grabbed my forearm. "Yeah, c'mon. I don't bite."

Lagging behind, I sighed, "Okay."

When we entered the X-ray room, he looked at me. "You know what to do. I'll be back in a minute."

I removed my scrubs top. He walked back in. The ventilation in the room seemed dense. My chest rose and fell rapidly. We looked at each other. The dampness in my panties wasn't as obvious as the huge bulge in his slacks. I sucked in as much air as I could. Then, slowly, rhythmically blew it out. He spoke first. "Turn to the right."

I followed instructions, but an eternity passed between each shot. Visions of him inside of me invaded my mind. When he finished, I faced him and slowly licked my bottom lip.

He shook his pants leg out and covered his indecency with a clipboard. My body language invited him to enter me. He smiled and put his hand on the door. My eyes begged him not to leave. He swung his hair back. "Put your clothes on."

Shamed by my overactive hormones, I put my shirt over my head. What the hell was I thinking?

When I passed his office, he called me. I went to the door. "Laila, I'll do your adjustment next week. My schedule's a little busy today."

Without offering him eye contact, I nodded.

Jordan avoided me for the rest of the day. When it was time to leave, I grabbed my coat. Jordan came out of the office. "You hangin' out with me tonight?"

I shrugged my shoulders. "Do you want me to?"

He lifted my chin with his hand. "Didn't I promise you I'd show you the town?"

I nodded. He laughed. "All right then."

"Where we going?"

"There's a few places we can go. We can grab a bite to eat. Hit a little club or something."

I frowned. "A club?"

"Not necessarily a club. More like a lounge."

I shrugged. "Why not? I'm not doing anything else."

He pounded my hand. "Deal. I'll pick you up at eight." He mashed my hair. "Is that enough time for you to get glamorous?"

I nodded. "Yeah. That's enough time."

When Jordan arrived, I was already standing in front of the building. I jumped in the car. He smiled, "You smell good."

Looking straight ahead, I said, "Thanks."

I folded my arms. He chuckled. "Why are you so closed off tonight?"

Obviously still offended, I pulled my lips in tightly and shrugged my shoulders.

He laughed. "Laila, you're something else."

I rolled my eyes. He laughed again.

He put his hand on my bare knee. "It's kinda cold for that short skirt."

I didn't respond.

"You got on your get-'em-girl boots."

He continued to amuse himself. I stared out of the window. Finally, he pulled up in front of a restaurant called Bluzette. He pointed. "Go ahead in and put our name on the list."

The aroma enticed me when I opened the door. My stomach rejoiced. By the time Jordan came in, the hostess was calling my name.

Jordan laughed. "Jackson, huh?"

I nodded. He shook his head. "Don't you know that you're always supposed to put the table in the man's name?"

I shook my head. "No, I never knew that."

White linen tablecloths covered the tables and white seat covers draped over the chairs. Small tea-light candles decorated each table. The atmosphere created a romantic vibe. The hostess took us to a table for four, one side a booth, the other two chairs. I slid into the booth. Jordan scooted in beside me, practically pushing me to the wall. I adjusted my skirt.

He looked at me. "Are you okay?"

I smiled. "Yeah, just a little cramped."

He moved over some. "I'm sorry. Do you want me to sit over there?"

"No, you're fine."

He raised his naturally arched eyebrows and blinded me with his bright smile. "You sure now?"

He proceeded to move out of the booth. "I can just move right over . . ."

I grabbed his forearm. "Jordan, sit down."

He laughed. "Okay, if you force me, I'll stay."

I patted his knee and batted my eyes. "Please."

He gazed into my eyes. "I like that."

I smiled. "What?"

"Your sensitive side. I didn't think you had one."

I covered my chest with my hand, "Me?"

He nodded. "You."

"I think I'm very sensitive."

"You might be, but I haven't seen that side of you."

The waitress came and broke up our breakthrough. After we ordered, he faced me. "So, what were we saying?"

I shrugged my shoulders. He laughed. "See what I mean?"

I shook my head. "No."

"You're so distant."

I folded my arms on the table. "What do you want to know?"

"I want to know why you're so tough."

I stared at the candle and tapped my fingers on the table. "I'm not tough at all."

The waitress brought our drinks. Jordan unwrapped my straw and stuck it in my glass. I smiled. "Thanks."

He looked into my eyes. "What do you like to do?"

I shrugged my shoulders. "Nothing, really."

He shook his head. "What do I have to do to get you to say more than two words at a time?"

"I don't know."

He folded his arms. "Man, I can't get a whisper out of you."

I rapidly created this fabulous story of my life and how I arrived in Philly. "Okay. I'm going to answer all your questions. I'm twenty-two. I grew up with just my grandmother and me. For the last three years, she was sick. I pretty much spent most of my good years taking care of her, so I haven't done much." I shrugged my shoulders. "I don't even know what I like to do. She recently died. So I decided to come here for a change of scenery."

He looked surprised. I could tell he regretted being so pushy. "I'm sorry to hear that. When did she die?"

"Two months ago."

"What was wrong with her?"

Our food came, which gave me an opportunity to straighten out the facts of my fictitious story.

I quickly commented on the food. He rapidly returned to his question. I fumbled with my napkin and said. "Cancer . . ."

"What kind?"

Shit. He was too damn inquisitive. "Um . . . lung." I took a big scoop of macaroni and shoved it in my mouth. I confirmed, "Yeah, lung cancer."

He took a bite of chicken. "Did she smoke?"

I nodded. He shook his head and said, "Cancer is no joke."

I took a deep breath and stared at the ceiling. "Nope."

"So you really haven't lived, huh?"

Praying that he was done with the cancer question, I shook my head cautiously. "Not really."

"You don't have any siblings, cousins?"

I shook my head. "Just me."

"What about your parents?"

I squirmed. "My mother was an only child and she died of an overdose when I was one, so I never knew her. No one ever knew my father."

His eyes popped out. "Wow. No wonder you're so tough."

I shrugged my shoulders. "I guess."

Still baffled as to how someone could have no family, he asked. "I mean, you don't have any distant relatives?"

"Nope. My grandmother didn't deal with anyone. I don't know where to begin."

He shook his head. "So, by the time you were eighteen, you had more responsibility than the average adult." He looked at me in amazement.

I nodded. "Pretty much."

The questions about my past finally ended and we had a pleasant dinner as I embarked on the future. By the time dessert arrived, we were stuffed. We looked at each other. Then, at the dessert. We both laughed.

He took a spoonful of bread pudding and offered me some. I gladly opened my mouth. "You sure can eat for someone all of 110 pounds soaking wet."

I covered my mouth. "Leave me alone."

"I'm just playin'."

By the time the check came, we were sitting there like two overstuffed turkeys. Both, breathing deeply. Our eyes wandered around the restaurant.

He ran his knuckle over my sideburns. "You're so hairy."

Feeling rather self-conscious, I nodded.

"It's pretty though."

He paid the bill and we waddled out of the restaurant. He wrapped his arm around me to shield me from the cold air. I tucked my chin inside my jacket. He bent down and kissed my forehead.

"Did you have a nice time?"

I nodded.

"Me, too."

CHAPTER 8

I hoped Jordan would call, but he didn't. The weekend passed and I found myself constantly making love to my Jordan pillow. Never have I found such a pale man attractive, but he obviously had cast a spell on me.

When he walked in the office on Tuesday morning, I popped up like jack-in-the-box. "Hey, Jordan."

He casually hugged me. "What's up, sweetheart?"

I smiled. "Nothing."

He bent down and hugged Ann. "Hey, lady."

He handed Ann a Burger King bag. He looked at me, "Did you eat yet?"

I nodded. "I figured that." He pulled a slice of cheesecake from his bag. "Here. I got dessert for you."

I blushed. "Aw. Thank you."

He shook his head. "Ain't nothing, baby."

When Jordan walked to the back, Ann looked at me suspiciously. "Somebody's got a crush."

Surprised that I was so obvious, I raised my eyebrows. "Me?"

Ann coughed. "I'm talking about Dr. Maxwell. I think he has a crush on you."

I said, "Whatever. He's not thinking about me."

She folded her arms. "He wasn't this friendly with the last assistant."

I shook my head. "Ann, I think you're seeing things."

Jordan called for me, "Laila."

She smiled. "Go."

Pretending that I didn't want to run, I dragged into his office. Trying to appear professional, I said, "Yes, Dr. Maxwell?"

He winked. My eyes roamed. "Set up the room for your adjustment."

"Okay. Are you going to do it now?"

He nodded. "Yep."

When he came in to do my adjustment, the radio was playing Sade. I hummed to "No Ordinary Love."

"You sound so sweet."

I stopped and lowered my head. He lifted my chin with his hand. "Don't stop."

I shook my head. He laughed and pointed to the table. "Get on."

I lay on my stomach. He ran his fingers down my spine. Every nerve in my body paused. His forefinger and thumb pushed upward. The pressure seized my senses. I inhaled him as he hovered over me. His cologne made me high. My eyes rolled in my head. Desire seeped from the corner of my mouth.

He held my head and rotated my neck. I moaned. He stretched my arms out. "Take a deep breath."

I breathed deeply. His touch produced orgasmic responses. I seductively licked my lips. In this midst of my release, he stopped. "All done."

I could have lain there forever with his hands massaging every inch of my body. Instead, I slowly rose and sat on the side of the table. My equilibrium was unbalanced. The room spun around me. He smiled, "You okay?"

I nodded. "I just feel a little woozy."

He smiled. "I know that's real."

I frowned. "What?"

He smiled and massaged my shoulder. "My patients have reported they have occurrences of feeling that they were walking on air."

I pushed him. "Whatever, Jordan."

At quitting time, Jordan didn't make his usual offer. He rushed out. "I'm going to catch you ladies on Thursday."

He dashed out of the door. I stood in the middle of the waiting room, waiting. After he had touched me so sensually, I felt stranded.

Ann handed me my coat. I put it on slowly, hoping Jordan would run back and remember he promised to show me the town. I wrapped my scarf around my neck.

Dr. Ryder came to the front jingling his keys. "Are you ladies staying the night?"

We laughed. Ann grabbed the door. "I'm leaving now."

I lagged behind. Dr. Ryder turned off the lights. "Laila, I'll drop you off if you want."

I shrugged my shoulders. "Okay."

We stepped outside. He locked the door. The wind whipped my hair around. I tried to tuck my face further into my scarf. Dr. Ryder put his arm around my shoulder. I shivered.

We sat in the car. He put the key in the ignition and we sat there.

"So, are you getting settled?"

I nodded.

"Have you met any interesting people?"

"Not really."

"Hasn't Jordan been taking you out?"

"Yeah, but . . ."

"He's knows a lot of people."

I nodded.

"Get him to introduce you to some people. He knows a lot of girls your age."

I smiled. "I bet he does."

He pulled away. "Oh, not like that. He's just a friendly guy."

I nodded. "I understand."

"I told him that he should help you assimilate."

I sighed. Knowing that he was instructed to be nice to me was somewhat unflattering. My chin sank.

"Yeah, you guys are around the same age." He paused. "He's a little older than you, but you're probably into the same things. I'm sure you don't want to hang out with an old white guy."

Without explicitly denying it, I smiled. We pulled up to my building. He patted my leg. "See you in the morning."

The hours ticked slowly, as I awaited Thursday's arrival. When Jordan stepped through the door, I was fulfilled. He smiled. I batted my made-up eyes.

"Hey, Jordan."

He hugged me. "What's up, Laila?"

He dropped Ann's lunch on the desk and handed me cheese-cake. I opened the container. As I took a fork and dug a chunk of the cake, I commented on how good it smelled. I licked the piece atop my fork. Then, I inserted it in my mouth, attempting to awake every taste bud. As slowly as I inserted it, I slid the fork out of my tight lips. I moaned. "Ummmm."

My attempt to entice him was successful. He stared at me. His jaw slightly hung. "You make that look good."

I smiled. He mumbled, "Don't do that shit to me in the of-fice."

I rolled my eyes. "Whatever, boy."

Ann trotted to the front. "Hey, you."

He hugged her. "Hey, Ann."

He hustled to the back. I finished my dessert. Each time he passed me, he looked as if he would swallow me. I delighted in knowing my sex appeal was still alive. At quitting time, I awaited his question.

Like clockwork, he came behind me and massaged my shoul-ders. "Whatchu doing tonight?"

I shrugged my shoulders. He progressed to my neck. I ducked away from his touch. He chuckled. "You hangin' with me or what?"

I nodded. "Where we going tonight?"

As if he was embarrassed, he sighed. "Well Laila, I'm a poet."

Unconsciously, I smiled. Excited that we could establish a sense of commonality, I swung around and inadvertently spat out what I've never before admitted. "Me too."

He smiled. "Are you?"

I nodded. Like it was now cool, he boasted, "Yeah, I'm performing tonight at this spot. I mean, I usually perform weekly."

Perform? That was a stretch for me. I'd seen the whole *Love Jones* thing, but to actually read my poetry in front of a group of people was inconceivable. In awe that he could, my mouth hung open. "Really?"

"Yeah, do you perform?"

Hell, no! I yanked my neck back and slowly shook my head. Attempting to retract my claim, I said. "My stuff is more Dr. Seuss type poetry."

He turned his lips. "How do you know if you never read it aloud?"

I shrugged my shoulders. He pinched my cheek. "After we get in from the club, you'll have to share some of your work."

I smiled. Inadvertently, I agreed. "Okay."

"All right then."

When we walked into the club, most people had naturals. Feeling like I was in the midst of the Neo Soul Convention, I absorbed the culture. Jordan pulled out a chair for me. I sat down and he strolled away. As I sat uncomfortably scoping the room, people welcomed me. They casually walked past and everyone greeted me. Men and women. No reservations, just sincere hospitality.

"Hello, sister."

"Blessings."

"How are you, beautiful?"

Love was in the house. Jordan returned with a glass of wine. I whispered. "I don't drink."

He laughed. "A glass of wine won't kill you."

"Okay, if you insist."

I sipped. Various friends greeted him. He introduced me as his coworker. They all embraced me. When one girl hugged me, she said, "You're family now. I hope to see you again."

I've never been a member of anyone's family. Her words filled my eyes. Jordan looked at me, "Are you okay?"

I wiped my eyes and covered my mouth as if I'd just yawned. "Just tired."

Diverting attention from me, some guy yelled, "J. Maxx!"

Jordan stood to hug him. The guy said, "I hope you're reading tonight, man."

He looked at me. "Have you ever seen this man perform?"

I shook my head. He patted Jordan's back. "Well you're in for a treat tonight."

I smiled. "I bet."

He reached down and hugged me. "I'm Sundiata, the emcee."

I nodded. He said, "And you are?"

Jordan chimed in before I could answer. "This is my coworker, Laila. She's also a poet."

Sundiata asked, "Do you perform also?"

I quickly denied Jordan's statement, "I'm not really a poet. I just write for fun."

Sundiata rubbed my shoulders. "We'll have you on stage in no time."

I rolled my eyes. "If you say so."

He and Jordan laughed. I smiled. He walked away. The small lounge filled. Sundiata came to the stage. He greeted the crowd. He introduced the first poet. Her words immediately rumbled through the crowd. Her presence was dramatic, her message prolific. How could I ever read my cat-in-the-hat poetry?

As each poet came to the stage, my confidence slowly evaporated. Finally he introduced J. Maxx. The crowd roared. They snapped. They stood. Joining his fan club, I was on my feet, clapping.

Jordan smiled. He motioned for the crowd to settle, they obliged. He prefaced his reading, "The poem I'm about to read is about how brothers try to be good guys." He dramatically grabbed his heart. "But something . . ." Then he grabbed his crotch. "I mean, something."

The crowd burst into laughter. He looked down at his hand groping his nature. He squinted and shook his head. "Something keeps holding us down. Forcing us to make the wrong decision."

The crowd clapped. The inflection in his voice rose. "Ladies, we don't mean it though. This one's for you. It's called 'Silk on Sandpaper.'"

Jordan's poem was both entertaining and absolutely hilarious. He shared the thoughts of a man. It seemed to be in violation of brotherhood. Obviously not, because when he walked from the stage, dudes barked at him. The ladies shook their heads, but many still gave him hugs. When he got to the table, I stood to hug him. "That was so good, Jordan."

He nodded. "Thanks, baby. Now we gotta get you up there."

I shook my head. "I can't get up there."

He grabbed my hand. "Okay. I won't force you." He rubbed the top of my hand with his thumb. "For now, you can just share your poetry with me."

I rolled my eyes in my head. "Maybe."

He looked. "Maybe?"

I nodded. "Yes."

"You make a brotha work hard."

"It's not that. I just . . . I just don't feel comfortable sharing my poetry yet."

He raised his hand. "Okay, I'll leave it alone."

He pulled up to my building. He kissed my cheek. "Okay, Laila. I'll see you Tuesday."

The night seemed too short. Thoughts of loneliness paralyzed me. I sat motionless. He rubbed my thigh. "Laila?"

"Yes."

He waved his hand in front of my face. "Where are you?"

I sighed. "I'm here."

"You're daydreaming."

Fearing rejection, I decided not to ask if he wanted to come in. I grabbed the door. "Let me go. I have to get ready for work in the morning."

As if he read my mind, he grabbed my hand. "So, are you going to read for me?"

My frustration with sleeping alone forced me to nod anxiously and say, "Yes."

He rubbed my hand. "When?"

Without a second thought, I said, "Now."

Completely shocked by my response, his eyebrows shot to the sky. The corners of his mouth reached for his ears.

He swerved into a parking space. "Let's go!"

When we walked into the apartment, Jordan quickly made himself comfortable. He sat down before I offered. He tossed his coat on the arm of the couch. My notebooks were spread out on my bed. He stood up and grabbed one of my notebooks. I rushed over to take it from him.

He offensively raised his hands. "Oh I'm sorry. I guess I overstepped the boundaries."

I rolled my eyes. "Yes."

He sat down, stretched his legs out in front of him and folded his arms behind his head. He closed his eyes. "Whenever you want to get started, I'm listening."

Trying to give myself time to mentally prepare, I pulled a pair of sweatpants from the chest. I went in the bathroom and changed. After mouthing snippets of my poetry in the mirror, I finally walked out. Jordan appeared asleep. I tiptoed to him.

He whispered. "I'm waiting."

He startled me. I mumbled, "Here I come."

I paged through my notebook and selected a seductive poem. I knelt beside him and stuck a pen top in my mouth. After reading the poem silently, I sighed.

"Any day now."

I whined. "Okay. I'm coming."

He looked at me from the corner of his eye. "Don't say that."

I smiled and took a deep breath. It was the first time I'd shared my love. My poetry. Without further delay, I began. "This is really hard, but here it goes. 'Melodic Lust . . .'"

His eyes remained closed. He smiled. I removed myself from reality. Two lines into the poem, I was caught in the rapture of the words. Each one rolled so freely from my tongue. Alone in my world, I acted out. I touched my breasts. I twirled my hips. "Busting rhymes for this man inside of me."

I moaned. "Melodies afire . . ."

Jordan put his hand on my waist and massaged it. He slowly lifted my shirt and rubbed my stomach.

The poem heightened. "Music we made. Notes we played." I licked my lips and clamped my teeth together. As I pretended he was the person I described, my eyes fluttered. "Visions of the possibilities of us," I paused. Finally, as if he made me climax, I winced. "Shit. I came."

I put the book on the floor. Jordan put his lips on mine and mumbled, "That was good."

We kissed. His strong hands rubbed vigorously on my body. He leaned over me. My heart thumped. My pelvis filled. Desperately wanting him, I reached down and grabbed the bulge that plagued my thinking from the moment I saw it. He softly bit my neck and pulled off my shirt. I rubbed his back and put my hand inside of his pants. He kissed my face all over. Then, he covered my breast with his mouth. Slowly, he slid down, kissing every inch. With his tongue submerged in my belly button, he pulled my sweats down. I moaned. "Ooh."

He stood up and stared at my naked body, "Damn, you're fine as shit."

He ripped his jeans open and pulled his boxers down. I whispered, "Oh my God!"

Confirming my suspicions, his huge endowment stood proudly protruding from his chiseled body. Anticipation leaked from me. He grabbed a rubber from his pocket. Standing in front of me, he slowly, meticulously rolled the condom onto his beautiful structure. I sat hypnotized. He sat on the bed and reached for my arm. He pulled me to him. I climbed on. He attempted to enter me. My body resisted. I squinted. "Ouch."

Holding my hips, he guided me. He smoothly opened the deprived entrance. So many years since I'd been with a man I could feel. My eyes watered. I wrapped my arms around his neck. My knees submerged in the mattress, as I gyrated on him. He groaned as he pushed himself deeper inside of me. Pleasure and pain, my body indulged.

He rolled me over onto my back. His eyes opened wide, and his stride was intense. He grunted. I held his face between my hands. He kissed my fingers. I wiped his sweat and nibbled on his lips. We sighed. We moaned. We were in a moment free of judgment, full of lust.

CHAPTER 9

I turned over to find the fine man who fell asleep beside me missing. My heart dropped. I lay in my moistness alone. I sat up, rubbed my eyes. I yawned. The light from the bathroom glared on the wall. I mumbled, "Jordan."

I climbed out of the bed. With my arms crossed over my breasts, I tiptoed into the bathroom. Empty. Coat gone. Shoes gone. Keys gone. I sighed. Couldn't he have let me know he was leaving?

I stood alone in the middle of my apartment. My eyes watered. I wrapped my arms around my neck, longing for the affection of a man. I closed my eyes, took deep breaths, and paced in circles.

After taking a dose of my sleeping cocktail to silence the voices of insecurity, I crawled into my empty bed and quickly drifted into a deep slumber. Awakened by the cell phone vibrating on my nightstand, I rubbed my eyes. The numbers on the screen meshed together. My voice scratchy from too much wine, I answered, "Hello."

After building my hope that it was Jordan, I was disappointed to hear Dr. Freid's voice. I mumbled. "Hi, Dr. Freid."

"Well, you don't sound so happy to hear from me."

"I'm sorry. I'm just waking up."

He cleared his throat. "Really? I thought you had to be at work by nine."

My heart sank. "What time is it?"

"Eight forty-five."

I mouthed, "Oh shit."

"Did you oversleep?"

"Yeah." I popped up and scurried around the room, pulling out underclothes, socks, scrubs. "What's up?"

"I just wanted to let you know that David hasn't called me in the last couple of days," he chuckled softly. "So, I think the coast is clear."

I paused and closed my eyes. "I hope so."

"Laila, I hear you're doing well there. Be strong."

I nodded. "I will. I'll be strong."

Why wasn't I strong enough to resist Jordan? He broke my daydream. "Keep in touch."

"Okay. I will." I sighed. "Thanks again. I could never have done this without you."

He brushed off my gratitude as usual and hung up.

I rushed in the office fifteen minutes late. I ran into the back, "Dr. Ryder, I'm sorry."

He smiled gently, "Calm down, Laila. It's fine."

"It won't happen again. I just forgot to . . ."

He raised his hand. "Don't sweat it."

I blushed and folded my hands together. "Thank you."

He waved me out of the office. "Just don't let it happen again."

We both laughed. I strolled into the front with Ann.

She smacked her gum. "You had a long night. Huh, girlie?"

I shook my head. "Not really."

The wind chime rang. All eyes shifted to the front. I bit my bottom lip. Ann spoke. "Jordan, what are you doing here on a Friday morning?"

He walked in and put the Dunkin Donut bag and coffee down. He placed one hand on my shoulder and the other on Ann's. "Bringing breakfast for my favorite girls."

Ann's wicked laugh howled. "I thought I was your *only* girl."

He winked at me. Ann pushed him. He apologized. She laughed again. "It's okay. She is much younger and prettier than me."

To appease her, he pinched her cheek. "You know you're my only girl."

She twisted her lips. "I've been feeling neglected since Laila started."

Their petty conversation bothered me. I grabbed the bag. "Here, Ann."

Jordan ran his fingers through my hair. "Actually, Dr. Ryder needed some help today. So he asked me to pop in for awhile." He pointed at me as I distributed the food. "I got you eggs and cheese. Is that cool?"

I nodded and rolled a chair close to Ann's desk. I unwrapped my sandwich and Jordan stood behind me with his hands on my shoulders. My nerves danced anxiously. He and Ann exchanged small talk. I conversed with my alter ego. *It must have been good. He's up early in the morning, bringing me breakfast.*

Jordan vigorously rubbed his thumb and forefinger into my shoulder. Chills danced up my spine. I peeped at Ann. She winked at me. I shifted. He realigned. I shifted again. He stopped.

A patient entered and the air cleared. I quickly ran in the back to set up a room. On my way to the front, Jordan met me in the hall. His chest bulged in my face. I looked at him. "You're due for your second adjustment."

I curled my lips. He laughed and pushed an exam room door open. "Set up the room."

"Let me make sure Dr. Ryder is okay."

I checked on Dr. Ryder. He was in the middle of a physical therapy treatment. I looked at the clock and made a guess as to when he'd be done. I rushed into the exam room and sat down in a chair.

Jordan shuffled in shortly after. He stared at me. I asked, "Why did you leave last night?"

"I couldn't get comfortable."

I huffed. "Why didn't you tell me you were leaving?"

He walked over and stood in front of me. His midsection stared me in the face. My mouth watered. He ran his fingers down my jawline. "You were sleeping so peacefully."

I sucked my teeth. "Whatever."

He bent down and kissed my forehead. "Honestly."

He patted the exam table. "Go 'head. Hop on."

I hesitated. "You don't have to take your clothes off," he said. "I know."

He chuckled. "Not unless you want to."

I flared my nostrils. "I don't want to."

He raised his arms. "Okay."

I lay on my stomach. His hands connected with my hotspots. He calmed the sounds screaming from my spine. My pelvis pulsated. He put his cool hand under my shirt. I pretended not to be fazed. He tugged at the drawstring on my pants. I tilted to the side. He reached around with one hand to undo the knot and instructed me to stay facedown by putting his other hand on my back. Slowly, he pulled my pants to my knees. He stuck one hand in between my thighs and landed soft kisses on my back. He tickled my dampness. I tightly tucked my lips in to muffle my pleasurable sounds. He gently massaged my legs apart. My limbs were limp, as they hung from the table. His tongue stroked me. Softly. Deeply. Without missing a drop, his moistness swallowed my moistness. He unbuckled his pants. Anxious for him, I squirmed. He climbed on top of me. Slowly, he entered me. I moaned. The paper on the exam table crumpled. As it ripped in multiple spots, we readjusted. We chuckled. He covered my mouth. He drooled in the crease of my neck. My skin tingled as his dreadlocks dangled on the side of my face. The explosion inside was too pervasive to acknowledge the small irritation. Grinding slowly, breathing intensely, we basked in sexual ecstasy during work hours. When I unconsciously released sighs of fulfillment, Jordan softly whispered, "Shh . . ."

His sweat dripped on me, as he reached his threshold. Quietly and carefully, he rolled off me. "Don't move."

He grabbed sterile paper towels and gently cleaned me off. He chuckled. "I don't believe you got me all open."

He helped me to sit up and pull my pants on. I was ashamed when I looked at my wrinkled scrubs. As if he were the only one to blame for our indiscretion, I pushed him. "Oh my God! Jordan, look at me."

"You'll be all right."

I reached out to hug him. He gave me a quick pat on the back. "Hurry up. We gotta get out of here."

He walked out. I pulled the paper from the table. Cleaned the room. Hoping to dissolve the sex odor, I sprayed Lysol. Feeling suspicious, I cracked the door and peeped left and right. I walked into the hall and scurried to the front.

Feeling like I'd gotten away with it, I smiled. Ann rolled her eyes. I smiled again. She curled her lips. "You got a mark on your face."

I wiped my cheek. She glared at me. "You can't wipe it off. It looks like your face was pressed against something."

I didn't respond. Now, as if I had been caught red-handed, my heart pounded. I looked at the appointment book and rushed back to set up another room.

Shortly before lunch, Jordan walked out. "My work is done for the day."

Ann nodded. She smirked at me. "We know."

My eyes called out for him. He waved. "I'll see you pretty ladies on Tuesday."

I wanted to chase him. Instead, I stood, abandoned. I questioned his motive for coming into the office in the first place.

Ann shook me. "Don't worry, girlie. You'll see him Tuesday."

I nodded. "Yeah, I know."

It was obvious that Jordan and I needed to talk. I felt like a convenient mattress. I'd come too far to turn back to my old ways.

CHAPTER 10

Friday night passed. Saturday night passed. No more movies to watch. No more words to write. I lay in my bed Sunday morning and rummaged up the courage to call Jordan. His voicemail picked up. I left an upbeat message.

"Hey Jordan! It's Laila. Give me a call when you get the message."

When I hung up, I kicked wildly in the air. How could I be so stupid? I wrapped my entire body up in my covers. I wanted David. I needed his security. I needed to know he loved me more than life itself. I wanted to call him. I wanted him to promise me the violence would end.

I grabbed my cordless phone and dialed the first five digits of my old phone number. I bit my nails. I contemplated. Finally, I hung up.

My cell phone rang. It startled me. I dropped the cordless phone like it was a hot curling iron. Then, I picked up the phone by the antenna. I poked the talk button. Trying to appear calm, I said, "Hello."

"What's up?"

Gathering my thoughts, I paused. "Hi, Jordan."

"Hey. I was in church."

"Oh."

Suddenly, I realized I had nothing to say. Seemingly minutes passed. I felt pressured to speak. "I was just calling . . . hmm . . . cause . . ."

He laughed. "Laila, you don't need a reason to call me."

I sighed. "Thanks."

"I'm hitting the poetry joint tonight. You tryna go?"

I nodded. "Yeah. I really enjoyed it the last time."

"Are you going to read tonight?"

"No. I can't read my popcorn poetry in front of all those people."

"Laila, your poetry is far from popcorn. Your shit is intense."

"You think?"

"I'm gonna get you on that stage, if it's the last thing I do."

I laughed. "I'm glad you think so."

"I'll pick you up around eight. Bring your notebook with you."

Jordan banged on my door around 7:30. Wearing only a towel, I opened.

Although I was flattered to see him, I said. "You're early . . ."

He rubbed my bare shoulder. "I know."

I walked back into the bathroom. He followed. He stood behind me in the mirror. What a perfect combination! Vanilla topping towered over a chocolate drop. He wrapped his arm around my waist and rubbed my hair.

He bent down and whispered, "Laila."

My insides tingled. He kissed the back of my neck. He ran his tongue down my spine. I reached behind me and ran my fingers wildly through his dreads. I mumbled. "We gotta get ready to go."

He unwrapped my towel. "We got time."

I whined, "No, we don't."

He grabbed my breasts and bit softly on my shoulder. Watching his hand rub on my dark skin aroused me. I sighed and leaned into his arm. We posed together in my mirrors for moments before I swung around to face him. Fire blazed between us. We stood momentarily paralyzed, as we gazed into each other's eyes. He kissed my forehead. His hair tickled my face. He reached down to raise my hips on the sink. I wrapped my arms around his neck. His nose rubbed against mine. I smiled.

As if a bomb burst inside of him, he roared. "Damn, girl. Why you doing this to me?"

As if he really expected a response, I shrugged my shoulders. He backed up and unbuttoned his jeans. He smiled. "You're so fine."

Sitting elevated on the sink, a moment of discomfort surrounded me, as he stepped out of his pants. He pulled his sweater over his head. He put on a rubber. Boy, did he make responsibility seem so enticing. I squirmed.

He leaned up on me. He pushed. I pulled. He laughed. "What's wrong?"

I shook my head. He poked gently, "You should be used to him now."

He made another attempt. I retracted. He lifted my hips and slowly worked his way inside. I moaned. He traveled to places I didn't know existed. My head turned vigorously from side to side, amazed by his journey. As he went deeper into the forest, I howled. The back of my head smashed against the mirror. Steam rose up my back. I called his name. Then, I yelled his name. Finally, I called for my Lord. No one saved me. Abandoned in the wild, I was free.

He wrapped his arms around my shivering body. "You all right?"

I nodded. He kissed me. "You know you got me trippin'."

I pressed my lips together. "Whatever, Jordan."

He rubbed my face. "Why don't you believe me?"

Afraid that questioning would run him away, I shrugged my shoulders. "I don't know."

I got in the shower again. He washed off. Sexually satisfied, we laughed at nothing. On the way out of the door, he asked, "Are you going to bring your notebook?"

Obviously still high from my orgasm, I grabbed my notebook and rushed out of the door. In the elevator, I realized I was carrying my book of shame.

"Oh my God! I have the wrong notebook. I have to go back up."

He tried to grab the book from me. The door opened. He stood in the door, as we played tug of war with my notebook. He laughed. "C'mon Laila, poetry is poetry."

More serious than he realized, I struggled for my life. "No, I can't read anything in here."

"C'mon."

"No."

"Laila, you got to start somewhere."

My eyes watered. "Jordan, no. Let it go."

He released it, "Damn, you make me wonder about you."

I fell back into the elevator. The door closed. I didn't press the button. I felt stupid. Someday, I'd have to tell my story to someone. Why not share it with my only friend in Philly?

I pressed the open door button. He stood patiently by the door. I reached for his hand, "I'm sorry."

He apologized. "You don't have to read tonight. I shouldn't force you."

I looked into his eyes. "No, I want to. I think I'm ready."

If I could bare my body in front of a bunch of grimy men, I sure could bare my soul to a group of positive people. He held the door for me. "That's good, because I told Sundi to put you on for tonight."

I pushed him. "Why were you so sure that you could get me to read?"

"I saw the desire in your eyes when we went Thursday."

I rolled my eyes. "You are so pushy."

He opened the car door. "Why would you say something like that?"

Without responding to his rhetorical question, I sucked my teeth and sat in the car.

When we got inside the club, my heart began to race. I grabbed his biceps and cuddled close to him. "Jordan, I don't know."

He pulled his arm away and wrapped it around me. "You'll be fine."

I shook my head. "I don't know."

Sundi walked up to us. He shook Jordan's hand. He smiled at me. "So, is she ready?"

Jordan nodded. "Yep, she's ready."

Fright glaring in my eyes, I smiled sheepishly. Sundi looked at me, "Okay, we let the first timers go first."

I raised my eyebrows and tugged on Jordan's sweater. "First?"

He patted my shoulder. "Trust me. It's better. Get it over and done with and you can sit back and enjoy everyone else."

We sat down at a table. Jordan ordered two Chardonnays. "If you have a drink, you'll be a lot less nervous."

When the waitress returned with the drinks, I swallowed the entire glass within seconds. I quickly ordered another one. Slowly, inebriation came over me.

Sundi called me to the stage. He introduced me, "She's a shy southern belle. So, y'all show her love." He stretched his arm in my direction. "Her name is Laila, which means Dark Beauty."

Suddenly I felt ignorant and unaware. I never even knew my name had a meaning. Hoping to shake off my ignorance, I shrugged my shoulders.

People clapped, as it dawned on me I hadn't selected a poem to read. I stood. My knees buckled. Jordan patted my back, "Go ahead. It's all yours."

I nervously walked to the stage. I tripped on the first step. Afraid to look into the crowd, I looked at Sundi. He grabbed my hand. "I got you."

No one laughed. They sat silently, awaiting my words. Sundi adjusted the microphone. "I'll stay up here with you if you'd like."

I smiled. "I'm okay."

The crowd clapped. I took a deep breath. The stage, about the same as I recalled, but the eyes staring back at me, awaiting my performance were different. I flipped through my notebook. Before I could evaluate my decision, I spoke, "The title of my poem is 'Black Don't Bruise' . . ."

Some whistled, others snapped. I heard a girl yell, "I know that's real, sista."

I smiled and cleared my throat. "You can stomp me to the ground. Blackberries grace cement with darkened hues. You can yank me, spank me, spit me. Did anyone ever tell you, Black Don't Bruise?

"A gift from God. The chosen few . . ."

The crowd got hyped, as they assumed I was embarking on a poem about Black power. Quickly, my words turned to that of an abused woman, being beaten by her mate who rescued her from a world of sex and darkness. A man whom she felt she owed her life. I described how time after time, she returned to her abusive lover, because she thought God gave her that skin to endure his abuse. As the final line of the poem escaped my lips, the crowd sat stunned. Bottom lips hung so low, they could mop the floor. Disbelief plagued the face of some. Sympathy lurked in the eyes of others. When I finished, every living being in the club stood up. They clapped. They snapped. They whistled. They shouted words of encouragement. They welcomed me. They hit high fives as I stepped from the stage. People hugged me. For the first time in my whole life, I felt like I belonged, like I was family. My eyes watered.

Jordan opened his arms when I got to the table. He hugged me.

"See, I told you. You were fantastic."

In the entire two weeks away from David, it was the first time I felt free. I darted into the bathroom. When I pushed the door, I was surprised to find several women inside. One girl was clearly distraught. She embraced me. We wept together. She looked at me, "Are you still with him?"

I shook my head. She asked. "How did you get away?"

"I don't know. It took a long time."

Other women in the bathroom eavesdropped on our conversation. I wasn't afraid anymore. The burden was lifted. She looked at me in amazement. "I would have never had the courage to get up there and speak so freely about it as you. You're my hero."

Since we were spilling truths, I admitted. "Girl, they made me get up there. And I swear, it was by coincidence that I read that poem."

We laughed. Another girl chimed in, "Girl, you rocked the house. I'm glad you read that one."

I couldn't believe them. Were they just nice or did they really think I was good? Sincerely grateful, I nodded. I sighed. "Thank you."

Someone added. "No. Thank *you*."

They made me cry again. We gathered in a huge group hug. Who would ever think the words I scribbled on paper would bring me into a union like this?

On the ride home, Jordan was quiet. Then he finally asked, "Did you experience that yourself?"

I played stupid, "What?"

"The poem. All that stuff you said."

I nodded.

He frowned. "How? When? You're so young."

I nodded. "I know."

"Did you live with the guy?"

I nodded.

With a confused expression, he asked, "Where was your grandmother?"

I took a deep breath. "Jordan, I'm sorry."

He wrinkled his forehead. "For what?"

I tucked one leg underneath me and turned to face him. "Jordan, I came here to get away from him. There was never a grandmother or whatever I told you."

He chuckled as if to forgive me. "I knew there were some inconsistencies. But, it's cool."

He patted my knee. I continued, "I was with him since I was eighteen."

He made an indigestion face. "Eighteen? How old was he?"

"He was twenty-five."

"What did your family say?"

I paused. I started. "I . . ." I paused. I stared out of the window. "I don't have any family." My eyes watered. "I was a foster child."

"What about your foster family?"

I snapped. "What about 'em?"

He massaged my leg, as if to retract his question. I wiped my tears. It was so difficult to explain my life. My breathing got heavy, as I attempted to suppress the resentment inside of me. I could feel his discomfort. He didn't comment. He kept his eyes on the road.

I rubbed his hand. "It's okay. I'm used to it now."

He trod cautiously, "What about your real family?"

I chuckled and rhetorically asked, "My real family?"

He nodded. I sighed. "Don't know where to start. My mother checked into a hospital under a false name, gave birth and bounced. I don't have much to go on."

Jordan pulled up to my building. I looked at him. He looked at me. We stared in silence. His eyes lowered. "Laila, you're strong. Don't let anyone tell you differently. I'm glad you read tonight."

He leaned over and cupped my chin. He landed a wet kiss on my cheek. The locks popped up escorting me out of the car. Exposed. Vulnerable. I asked, "Are you coming up?"

He shook his head. "I need to rest tonight. I have to study all day tomorrow."

After I splattered my heart all over his car, he didn't have the decency to come up and hold me. I forced a smile and put my hand in his. "I'll see you later."

He nodded. Reluctantly, I pulled the handle. Slowly, one leg, then two, I stepped out of the car. I reached my hand in and waved good-bye. Finally, I closed the car door. After my drawn-out exit, he sped away. His spinning wheels splashed me with the grungy water from the gutter, as if I were trash.

CHAPTER II

When Tuesday arrived, I was reluctant to see Jordan. How could he abandon me when I needed him most? His bright smile preceded him when he came through the door. Disgusted by his joy, I rolled my eyes and walked into the back. He shared rapid small talk with Ann and rushed to the back after me.

The usual hug. The casual kiss on the cheek. The played-out shoulder rub. I huffed. As if he was clueless, he said "What's wrong, Laila?"

I shook my head and scurried out of the exam room. He followed. As we got closer to the front, the tension subsided. Ann raised her eyebrow. "You guys seem preoccupied this afternoon."

I shook my head. "I'm fine."

Jordan folded his arms. Each time I moved, his eyes shifted in my direction. He was as obvious as a cold sore. Agitated by his surveillance, I stopped, stretched my eyes wide. "What?"

He and Ann looked shocked. I stormed into the back. This time I was alone. The words couldn't be found. The questions bounced around my mind. Why couldn't he just come save me? I bit my nails. I tried to reason with myself. Laila, be calm. I took deep breaths. Jordan walked up cautiously. "Laila."

"Yes?"

He touched my shoulder. "Are you upset with me?"

"No. I . . ."

"You seem upset. What did I do?"

I folded my arms. "Nothing."

"I'm going to follow you around until you tell me what's going on with you."

I covered my face and slowly slid my hands down. "I don't know. I don't know what I'm doing. I don't know why I feel like this. I don't know."

He chuckled. "Talk to me, Laila. Say what's on your mind."

"It just seems like after I told you about my past, you . . ."

"I, what?"

"You seemed like you started trippin'."

He chuckled. "That was just two nights ago. How can you say I was trippin'?"

Too ashamed to admit, I smacked my lips. "You just . . . I don't know."

He hugged me. "I was tired, Laila."

For my sanity, I needed to believe him, but his shifting eyes warned me not to.

"It just seemed like you wanted to get away from me so fast that night."

He shook his head. "I was tired."

"You could have slept with me."

He nodded. "I know."

I huffed. "I don't even know how we got here."

He reached out for my hand. "I don't either. And I feel really bad about it. I just wanted to . . ." He paused. "I just wanted . . ."

I braced myself for the worst. "You what?"

"I wanted to get you familiar with the city. I didn't expect to sleep with you."

"You sure didn't turn it down."

He tried to hug me. I yanked away. "Laila, I'm sorry."

"Why would you do that to me?"

He huffed. He paused. He huffed again. Finally, he admitted. "I'm a man."

His honesty crashed into my chest. It sank. The disappointment forced my jaw to drop. I closed my eyes, as he locked down on the already unbearable dog bite. "I can't do this work thing."

My pride wouldn't let me crack. "Okay. I understand."

I headed out of the room. He grabbed my arm. "Laila, it has nothing to do with what you told me."

I shrugged my shoulders. "I believe you."

I was bitter. I felt used. I wanted to go home. Instead, I performed my daily duties with a smile.

Around five-thirty, a girl walked in. Ann stood up, "Oh my God! Tamia . . ."

She grabbed her hand and brought her over to greet me. "This is our new assistant, Laila."

She shook my hand. "Hi, Laila. Jordan's told me all about you."

Ann called for Jordan. He moseyed in from the back. He walked directly to Tamia. She kissed him. "Hey, baby."

I felt like he hummed a brick into my head. She rubbed his back. "Hey, honey. You been busy today?"

He shook his head. My eyes shifted from her lips to his. He never looked in my direction. "C'mon back."

The moment they were out of sight, I sat beside Ann. "Is that his girlfriend?"

She pursed her lips, "Well, she *was* his fiancée."

I swallowed. "I didn't know he . . ."

"Well, that's why she *was* his fiancée. Jordan likes women. She called the wedding off two weeks beforehand, because he slept with one of the dancers from his bachelor party."

How many times have I done that? I never thought about the woman on the other side. I sighed. "How did she find out?"

"I don't know. That was last summer. This is the first time I've seen her in a while. They're obviously working something out."

Sarcastically I added, "Obviously."

Just like he was working my body out forty-eight hours ago. They're all the same. Pain is pain. Too much pain for one girl to handle.

I passed Jordan's office. I heard loving giggles escape the room. He intentionally stomped on me. Why? How could he be so deceptive with that innocent smile God gave him?

When six o'clock struck, I rushed out of the office. I needed to scream. I had to cry. I wanted to fight. I decided to take two doses of NyQuil to soothe the pain.

CHAPTER 12

When I stepped out of my apartment the next morning, Jordan was standing there. "I'm sorry."

I shrugged my shoulders. "Jordan, if you just wanted to fuck me, I understand. You're not the first man who just wanted to fuck me."

"I didn't know she was coming to the office."

I walked briskly past him. "Jordan, you made yourself clear before she even came. Her coming just put the cherry on top."

He tried to grab my hand. "I didn't make myself clear. I really like you, Laila."

I walked faster. "You like me. You like fucking me. Say that. You didn't stop until you got me just where you wanted me."

He accused. "You wanted it too."

I didn't respond. His toes to my heels, he tramped behind.

"I let my dick do something I don't believe in."

I smirked. "What is that, Jordan?"

"Fuck someone I work with."

I chuckled. "You didn't seem too apprehensive to me."

"I wasn't. Not until I felt all that tension at work yesterday."

I shook my head. "Whatever."

"You came to work with an attitude for no reason. I can't deal with that type of shit at work."

I stopped abruptly. "Okay. So why are you following me?"

He threw up his arms. "Pardon the hell out of me for trying to be polite."

I laughed. "You're excused."

I proceeded to walk away from him. He grabbed my arm. "Laila, look! Let me explain."

His fingers dug into my biceps. Shocked by his aggression, I frowned. I clenched my teeth. "Jordan! Let my arm go." I stared into his eyes. "I got your point."

He reluctantly freed me. The distress in his face reached out to hold me. I dropped my head and walked away. After a few seconds passed, I peeped over my shoulder. The distance between us grew. Suddenly, he was out of sight. I felt alone and lonely. As I stood there watching remnants of his presence disappear before me, he called my cell phone. I was too offended to answer. After five repeated attempts, he finally left a message. His voice trembled, "I was wrong. I should have never led you on. It just happened so fast. And I . . . I don't know what to say. We have to work in the same office and it's going be hard." He sighed. "Can we talk when you get off?" He paused. "Call me back."

I stood in front of the office, contemplated calling him back. My body burned for David. At least I knew he was mine. Ann opened the door.

"Why are you standing out here like you can't open the door?"

I smiled. "I don't know. I have a lot on my mind."

I walked sluggishly behind her. "Laila, you just don't seem like yourself today."

I sank into a seat in the waiting area. "I'm tired. I'm really tired."

I dropped my head in my hands. Why was I even here? I went from the storm into a hurricane. Problems seem to surround me wherever I go.

"You want some coffee?"

I chuckled. Ann took the literal interpretation of my fatigue. "Yeah, I'll have some coffee."

"I'm going over to Dunkin Donuts. You want a breakfast sandwich?"

I shook my head. She grabbed her coat. "I sure hate it when Jordan doesn't come in."

I wished Jordan could disappear. He seemed so sincere, only to turn out to be a liar. As I stared off into a dream world, Dr. Ryder walked in.

"Good morning, Ms. Laila."

I straightened my posture. "Good morning."

He sat on Ann's desk and dropped his briefcase on the floor. He smiled. "How's everything going?"

I nodded. "Okay."

He looked into my eyes. "You and I haven't had much time alone since you started."

I nodded. "Um-huh."

Ann opened the door. He suspiciously jumped up. He shook his pant leg out. It appeared that he was aroused, but I suppressed the thought.

"Good morning, Doc."

She sat the cup carrier on the desk. Dr. Ryder spoke and picked up his briefcase. He winked at me. "We'll talk later, kid."

He walked into the back. Ann sat down. "Be careful."

I raised my eyebrow. "You have to watch him," Ann said.

I chuckled. "Who?"

"Dr. Ryder. He's fresh."

Fine damn time to post warning signs. What happened to the one that said,"Beware of Jordan." I said, "They all are."

She laughed. "You got a point."

I agreed to meet Jordan at Hard Rock Café on Market Street. I rushed home to change, in hopes that when he saw me, he'd change his mind.

When I walked in, I spotted him sitting at the bar. I paused. Then, I proceeded. He pulled out the stool beside him. He stared at me, as I took small, concentrated steps toward him. Then, he injected the poison. His smile paralyzed me. Trying to cast away his spell, I blinked. Still, my heart fluttered.

Before I could sit, he said, "Thanks."

I nodded. He smiled. "I'm glad you were willing to meet me."

The bartender asked, "What are you drinking?"

I curled my lips and responded, "Long Island Iced Tea."

Jordan put his fist up to his mouth, "Whoa! I thought you didn't drink. What's up with that?"

I rolled my eyes. "People can drive you to drink."

"Don't make me feel bad."

"I'm not trying to make you feel bad."

He rubbed my forearm. "I already do."

I snatched my arm away. He shook his head. "I'm serious, Laila. I feel really bad."

I smirked. "Why is that? You got what you wanted."

He turned his body to face my side profile. I focused on the bartender. His knees pressed into my thigh. "I didn't want this."

The bartender set my drink in front of me. Jordan confirmed, "Put that on my tab."

Almost afraid to sip, I stirred my drink with the straw. He asked, "What was I saying?"

I shrugged my shoulders. He placed his hand on my thigh. I snatched my leg away. "Why you trying to make this hard?"

I rolled my eyes in my head. What about how hard it is for me? I sucked my teeth. How selfish could he be? He huffed. "This is not how I wanted it."

I snapped. My neck rolled. "What did you want?"

"I just wanted to bring you out of your shell. I didn't expect the sexual attraction to be so strong," he admitted. "After you read your poem, I knew that I had to end it."

I took a long sip. "Why then?"

"Because I knew that you were more sensitive than you originally let on." He paused. "I know I'm not ready for a relationship and I . . ."

"You just wanted to fuck me. Why can't you just say it?"

"Nah, I like you, Laila. That's why I'm doing this. I like you and I know I can't be what you need right now. After what you have been through, you need a good man, a dude that's going to be all about you. If I didn't care about you, I wouldn't be doing this. I swear."

Finally, I faced him. "Jordan, good men only exist in fairy tales."

He twisted his lips, "What?"

"You heard me."

He laughed. "Stop playin'."

I looked into his eyes. "I don't believe there's such a thing."

Confusion covered his face. Acceptance patched up my heart. I understood him. He failed to understand me. We ate. We made a friendship pact. We parted.

CHAPTER 13

It took two weeks of Jordan's coaxing before I returned to the stage. Afraid of our chemistry, I refused to go with him. I knew we'd end up romping around my little apartment. So, I found the courage to go alone.

I strutted up to Sundi. "Hi, remember me?"

We embraced. "Of course, Laila. We missed you the last couple of weeks. People have been asking about you."

I blushed. "Really?"

"Yeah, you have a fan club."

I playfully hit his arm. "I don't believe you."

"I'm serious. I asked Jordan about you. He said you probably weren't coming back."

I nodded. "I guess he was wrong."

He shook my hand. "I'm glad he was wrong. Are you bringing us something tonight?"

I nodded. "Yep."

"Do you still want to go first?"

I shrugged my shoulders. "It doesn't matter."

He patted my back and laughed. "You're a veteran now, huh?"

I nodded and found a small table alone. A waiter took my drink order. My new drink of choice was Long Island Iced Tea. By

the time Jordan graced us with his presence, I was cheerfully intoxicated. He bopped over to me. "Why didn't you tell me you
were coming tonight?"

I giggled. "I didn't know I was supposed to tell you."

"You're right, but I'm glad to see you."

He removed his hand from the seat. Behind him comes
Tamia. My excitement dampened. She stretches her arms out.
"Oh Laila, I'm glad to see you. Jordan told me the last time you
really did a good job."

I smiled. "Thanks."

They sat at a table across from me. My intentions were to read
a basic love poem. I decided to read the poem that I wrote about
Jordan. I snickered at the thought.

After the newcomer blessed us with his words, Sundi winked
at me. I was ready. I missed the love. I inched to the edge of my
chair. He introduced me. People stood as I walked through the
lounge. I nodded in appreciation as I stepped on stage.

I prefaced the poem, "Sistas, y'all can relate to this one."

They clapped. I blushed. "Y'all know. We try to make love out
of one night stands."

I giggled. "Once we set our eyes on a guy," I beamed at Jordan
and smirked, "if he gives us the slightest response, he's our
boyfriend."

I laughed. "So, let me see if y'all feel me." I smiled. "Bit, Bang,
Boom!"

I peeped at Jordan. As I noticed his discomfort escalate, my
confidence skyrocketed. In poetic terms, I described the Bit; the
initial attraction, the unspoken words, the failure to establish the
basis of the relationship. I proceeded to the Bang; the lies, the
entrance, the reception, the high, the anything goes. Finally, I
reached the Boom; the reality, the truth, the "It wasn't supposed
to be this way," ultimately leading to the end of a five-day saga.

I smiled and looked into the crowd. Jordan had sunk down in
his chair, while the rest of the room stood to their feet.

Sundi stepped on stage. "Laila shocked us with that one."

I winked as I passed Jordan. Tamia noticed the silent communication, just as I intended. I sat down and ordered another drink. I watched every move of the now disturbed couple. Jordan was antsy. Tamia was curious. I reveled in my revenge.

Suddenly, my weakness for an attractive man stood at my table; tall, dark, and handsome. "Somebody sitting here?"

His voice was deeper than the sea, rougher than sandpaper. My eyes shifted from side to side. I anxiously shook my head. He pulled the chair out and sat down. Big diamond studs in his ears, low haircut, a huge platinum cross around his neck, Timberland boots loosely laced, he didn't look like a regular.

As I stared at the stage, I felt his eyes on my back. He said literally five words to me the entire night, "Want something else to drink?"

I shook my head. That was the end of our conversation. I turned around when Jordan finished reading to gather my things. My weakness was gone. Damn. I should have said something else to him. I quickly labeled him the mystery man.

Both Jordan and Tamia passed without saying good-bye. I moseyed out slowly behind them. I bundled up, just in case recruiting a taxi took longer than expected. As I stood in front of the club, people pulled out of the parking lot. Finally, a girl who I'd remembered from the last time pulled in front of me.

"Laila, you need a ride, girl?"

I nodded.

"C'mon. Get in."

I sat in her car. "Thank you so much. What's your name again?"

"Danielle."

"I really appreciate this, Danielle. I live on Spruce Street, between Thirteenth and Fourteenth."

"Where you from?"

"Miami." I paused. "South Florida."

"Your accent is so cute."

I smiled. "Thanks."

"How long you been here?"

"About a month . . ."

"What made you leave Miami?"

I chuckled. "A sorry man."

"Not the guy you were talking about in the poem last time."

I nodded. "That's him."

"You mean you just left that guy a month ago?"

I nodded. She began to ramble about her boyfriend. "Girl, that poem was so deep. See, my man ain't abusive. He's just possessive as hell."

"Whatchu mean?"

"Girl, if he met you, he'd swear I was fucking you."

I laughed. "Yeah, my boyfriend." Just as I claimed him, I remembered I was free. "I mean, my old boyfriend was the same way."

"That shit is nerve-racking!"

I nodded. "Trust me. I know."

She curled her lips. "If I ain't had no kids by his insecure ass, I'd leave him."

I hissed. "If he ain't beating you, you might as well deal with it."

She sucked her teeth. "I don't know about all of that."

"They're all crazy."

She gave me a high five. Her midlength dreads flung from side to side as she accentuated each word. "You ain't never lied. And I got the nerve to have that fool's kids."

"Ain't nothing wrong with that."

She laughed. "You right."

She pulled out a picture of her kids. "That's Shandi and Jacob."

On the picture, her hair didn't have the fire red tips. I looked at the photo. Then back at her. "I like your hair with the red tips."

"This is something new."

She put the picture back in her purse. "You are so right. They're all crazy."

I laughed. "It's true."

"My man always tells me that it's a man's world. So, deal with it."

"No, he don't!"

We cackled and male bashed for several hours. It was two in the morning when we finally parted. She looked at the time. "Girl, he gonna have a fit when I get home."

We laughed and exchanged numbers. I barely closed the door before she sped off. I smiled. It may be true that when something is taken away, it gets replaced with something better.

CHAPTER 14

Weeks passed. Jordan's friendship slowly seemed to deteriorate. I wanted something from him that he couldn't offer. So, I began to resent him. We exchanged small talk, but never what I wanted to hear. I was glad when he turned in his resignation. He went to an office in North Philly. At least I didn't have to be reminded of what I couldn't have every day. Although at least once a week, I had to watch him bless the mike with his rhythmic words. His smooth tone always reminded me of his smooth moves. It rewound me back to the way his gifted hands blessed my needy body. Often, I found myself daydreaming while he stood on stage. When my eyes got glossy, Danielle would always shake me. "Shake it off, boo. Jordan ain't no damn good."

I always thanked her for bringing me back to reality and we'd laugh like teenagers. She had become my partner in crime. We strolled in the club every week together. For the first time in my life, I accepted something I used to shy away from, a good female friend. When we chatted all evening, I often wondered how I was able to survive so many years without a good homegirl.

After twenty-three years, I was finally becoming acquainted with Laila. Each week, I'd bring forth something new, something enlightening. I looked forward to being on stage. Whenever I spoke, I winked at Jordan, a sign of my gratitude. He responded by raising his glass to me.

With the birth of spring, freshness filled the air. My hair grew almost as fast as the flowers bloomed. I ran my fingers through my short bob, as I skipped home to prepare for my guaranteed weekly outing.

As always, Danielle beeped the horn and my home phone rang around eight sharp. I grabbed my keys and ran down the stairs.

When I got in the car, her eyes were puffy. She looked at me. "Ray-Ray is crazy."

I reached my arm around her. "I'm sorry. What happened?"

"He wants me to stop going to the club every week. You know he thinks I'm fucking somebody."

I sighed. "Whatchu gon' do?"

"I don't know."

She didn't talk about it for the remainder of the ride. I didn't pry.

Whenever I walked into the club, people raised their hands for high fives. I was always sucked into a whirlwind of greetings before I stepped on stage. No matter where I was in the lineup, there was never enough time to chill before I spoke. Danielle would always sit back and let me work the crowd.

When I got off the stage, I looked for her. She wasn't at the table. She wasn't in the bathroom or at the bar. She was nowhere to be found. I walked outside. Her car was gone from the parking lot. I was frazzled. Did she leave me? As I walked back into the club, I checked my cell phone. No messages. I called her. No answer. I stood near the door.

The mystery man walked up to me. Expecting the usual head nod, I smirked. Instead, he handed me a drink. I frowned. He smiled. Oh my God! I didn't think he was capable of forcing a smile. My forehead wrinkled. He said, "You drink Long Island. Right?"

I looked at the glass suspiciously. "Yeah."

He laughed. "I just wanted to get you a drink. Is that okay?"

I handed the drink back to him. "I'm not thirsty."

He laughed. I found out he had a sense of humor. He shook his head. "Maybe that was the wrong approach. Let's start over. Hi, my name is John."

I extended my hand. "And I am . . ."

We spoke simultaneously: "Laila."

He chuckled again. His teeth were beautiful. I never knew who hid behind that arrogant look. He made me smile. He nodded. "I know your name. I come here every week to hear you speak."

Flattered, I covered my heart with my hand. "Me."

He laughed again. "Yeah, you."

I squinted. "Then why haven't you ever said anything to me?"

"I speak to you."

I corrected him. "No, you give me a head nod." I shrugged my shoulders. "Like what does that mean?"

He laughed. "I'm feeling you."

"Feeling me?"

He amended his statement. "I'm feeling what you do on that stage."

It was thrilling to be admired for my brain and not my body. But for some distorted reason, I wanted the opposite from him.

As much as I was enthralled in our conversation, my eyes concentrated on the door. He added. "You got that hot shit."

I laughed. "What?"

He repeated. "That hot shit."

Flattered by his words, but preoccupied with the whereabouts of Danielle, I nodded. He clarified his statement. "I mean you can flow. The way you manipulate words is crazy. Your stuff is hot."

I tucked my lips in and shrugged my shoulders. "Thanks. I guess."

He nodded. "Definitely. I wanna give you my card. I need you on my team."

I chuckled. "Your team?"

He reached in his pocket and grabbed a card. "I own a record label. I'm a producer. If I add some beats to your joints, you'd have a bangin' CD."

I raised my eyebrows. "You think?"

He held onto my hand as I accepted his card. "Poetry is music and you're a damn good poet."

I nodded. "Thanks."

"Do you have a number?"

I nodded. "Um-huh."

He laughed. "Are you in another world or something?"

"No. I'm just looking for my girl."

"The one you're always with?"

I nodded. He pointed to the door. "I saw her rush out of here a little while ago. I think you were on stage."

"Was she alone?"

"Yeah." He raised one eyebrow. "Do you think everything's okay?"

I shrugged my shoulders. He smiled. "You want me to help you find her."

"Um . . . she'll be back. I'll just wait here."

He looked at his diamond-studded watch. "It's getting kinda late. What if she doesn't come back? How will you get home?"

How did he know I didn't have my own car? Noticing the inquisitive look on my face, he laughed. "I see y'all come in here every week and she's always the one driving."

I nodded. He shrugged his shoulders. He held the door open. "Let's go. We can either go somewhere to look for your girl or I'll take you home. Your choice."

I didn't move. I didn't respond. He said, "I don't bite."

As I realized I could possibly be stranded, my legs pushed my stubborn body towards the door. He smiled. "Why do you look scared?" He joked. "I'm trying to help you out."

I curled my lips. "I was taught not to talk to strangers."

"You see me every week. I'm not a stranger."

I curled my lips. "I didn't even know your name until five minutes ago."

"That's cause I try to stay on the low."

When we got into the parking lot, I noticed Danielle sitting in her car. "There she is."

Though she looked frantic, I was relieved to see her. John said. "So you don't need me now."

Apologetically, I smiled. "Not really."

He opened his arms. "Can I at least get a hug for my efforts?"

I nodded and wrapped my arms around his chiseled torso. Unconsciously, I rested my head on his protruding chest. Uh! The touch of a man. I almost forgot about Danielle. He backed up.

"Call me if you need me."

I nodded. I walked toward Danielle's car. He got into an ivory Cadillac Escalade. His wheels were chromed out. His music blasted through the speakers the moment he turned the car on. His head bobbed to the rhythm. I smiled at him and sat in Danielle's car.

"What happened?"

She shook her head. "Nothing, girl. Just be glad you don't have any kids."

"Why? What did he do?"

"He dropped them off at my mother's. He left the baby with no milk or Pampers. I had to rush over there to take her some milk. I didn't want to leave you stranded. That's why I came back."

"You didn't have to. I would have found a way home."

The crowd started pouring out of the club. She said, "I guess it's over."

I nodded. She peeped around me. "So what's up with mystery man?"

"He just started talking to me. I don't know what's up with him. He owns a record company. He wants me to make a poetry CD."

She was ecstatic. "For real?"

I nodded. She pushed me to transfer some of her excitement to me. "Are you?"

I sucked my teeth. "Girl, I don't know. I'm not trying to make a CD."

"Girl, you've had your eye on him for weeks. Now, you got your way in there."

I shook my head. "I don't know. I'm scared."

"What the hell are you scared of? We're grown."

I laughed because I knew I sounded silly. Before we pulled out of the parking lot, John drove back around and blocked us in. He left his car running, and hopped out. He walked around to the passenger side and handed me a pen and a napkin. "I didn't get your number."

I looked at Danielle. She smiled. I swiftly scribbled my info down.

He folded the napkin and put it in his back pocket. "I'll talk to you later."

The moment I got settled in bed, my cell phone rang. I answered. "What's up?"

His ashy voice was easily identifiable, "Hi. John. You made it home safely."

"Yes," I said.

"Everything cool with your girl?"

"Yeah, you know how baby daddies trip."

"Not all baby daddies trip. Do you have any kids?"

"No."

"That's good shit."

"Do you?"

He proudly responded. "Yep, one little man."

"That's cool."

"Yeah, I love him to death, too. So, what's up with you? You got a man?"

Again, I had to spell out the commercial story as to how I ended up in Philly alone. John bragged a lot, rarely asked questions, but seemed relatively considerate. He tried to recruit me to the studio. I promised him that I'd visit over the weekend.

CHAPTER 15

My phone rang early on Saturday morning. With my eyes stuck together, gook in the corners of my mouth, I answered, "Hello."

"What's up, homie?"

"John!"

He laughed. "Wake up."

I looked at the clock. "It's eight o' clock."

"Long night?"

I blushed. "No."

"Well, wake up. Do you want breakfast?"

"Um . . ."

"Get up, brush your teeth, and meet me at the Amish Market."

"Um . . ."

"I'll meet you there at nine. Peace."

He hung up. I sat up in my bed, stunned by his confidence. I rubbed my eyes. Could I be dreaming? I touched myself. I browsed the call log on my phone. It was real. I hopped out of my bed. I drifted back and forth from the bathroom to the window. Could he really be interested in me? Why had he waited so long to approach me?

I stood drowsily in the shower. The water revitalized me as it streamed down my face and through my hair. I fantasized about John. I scrubbed my delicate skin with a reviving aromatherapy scrub from Bath & Body Works. After almost twenty minutes, I turned the shower off and said a short prayer. "Lord, let him want me. I'm lonely. I'm tired."

I put on my ripped jeans and a black fitted T-shirt with the slogan, "My Boyfriend's Out of Town." I hoped the shirt would be a conversation piece. I added a little styling gel to the curly bush that sprouted all over my head. My color was slowly fading. My small silver studs gave me the dainty effortless look. I dabbed clear lip gloss on my lips. I put a light coat of mascara on my lashes. Early morning was no excuse to miss the bus I've been waiting on for two months.

Ten minutes to nine, I put on my short denim jacket that hit right beneath my breasts. I darted out of my building, jogged down Spruce Street, over to Twelfth Street, down Market Street. My bracelets jingled. My forehead was damp. I breathed. Slow down. He'll be there. I looked at my watch, 9:05. I reduced my pace. My moist hand on the market door, I took a deep breath. My phone rang.

"Where are you?"

"I just walked in. Where are you?"

"I see you."

He hung up. I twirled in a circle. Amish people surrounded me. John was nowhere in sight. Suddenly, I felt him behind me.

"What's up?"

I turned slowly. "Hi."

"You ever ate here before?"

"No."

"I eat here every Saturday morning. I like to start my day off fresh."

He pointed. "Their food is bangin'." Speaking with his hands, he continued, "Big huge eggs. Bacon. Whatever you want."

He rubbed his belly like a kid. "I love it." He laughed, "I guess you can tell I like to eat."

I nodded.

"Whatchu want?"

"Um. Eggs and bacon. I guess."

"We got a long day. You better get a big breakfast."

I ignored his inclusive statement. We sat at a high table. He helped me get situated. His actions, platonic. His conversation, friendly. The look in his eyes, innocent. Not even a mere implication. My writing seemed to be the center of his attraction.

"So I'm gonna take you to the stu and let you see how we vibe."

I chuckled. "The stu?"

He smirked. "The studio."

I nodded. "I see." I joked, "So, you're going to take me to the stu."

"C'mon now." He curled his soft charcoal lips. "Yeah, I want you to hang out. Listen to a few of my beats and see how you feel about putting some of your work to it."

I shrugged my shoulders. "Okay."

He added, "Let me warn you, I got a lot of artists that hang around. They're gonna be all over you."

What about you being all over me? I pursed my lips and waved my hand. "Whatever."

"But don't worry about them. You got work to do."

"John, I don't know if I'm really down for this."

He put his hand over mine. "Laila, I've watched you for months. You need to make yourself heard to a grand audience."

"So, why did it take you so long to say something?"

He smiled. "I'm selective. I'm real selective." He leaned closer. "Everybody can't be a part of the team."

I raised one eyebrow. "Okay, how do you know I can be a part of that team?"

He nodded. "I know."

When we walked out to his car, he opened the passenger door. He lifted me by the waist and helped me into the truck.

After he got in, he asked, "How long is your boyfriend going to be out of town?"

I laughed. "It's just a shirt."

"You gonna be in trouble wearing that in the stu. I'm telling you now."

Bright and early on a Saturday morning, the studio was full of dudes. I finally found out where all of the fine black men in Philly hang out. Guys were stretched out on couches, sitting on stools. They were everywhere. When I walked in, some stood up, some followed. I felt like the last chicken wing that had to be split amongst everyone. They licked their chops. They made insinuating grunts. John introduced me to his right-hand man. "This is Laila. She's that poetry chick I've been telling you about."

Poetry chick? What an endearing introduction. His friend nodded. Didn't offer to shake my hand and basically ignored my existence. I sighed. John laughed. "These dudes are crazy. Don't take them too serious."

I curled my lips to one side, "Yeah, you said that before."

He blushed and shook his head. "I run this show. Don't trip off nothing. If somebody offends you, lemme know."

I frowned. "Okay."

"I want to keep you around. I like your style."

Four hours into my day at the studio, my head was banging. The music blasted. Every guy that came in asked for my digits. They engaged in guy talk. I twiddled my fingers. I scribbled pictures on the notepad that I was given to write on. Didn't know if or when I should ask to go home. So, I waited. And waited. Finally, after a full day, John asked, "You ready, homie?"

I nodded. He reached his hand out to pull me up from the sunken couch. I looked into his eyes. He turned his head. He asked, "You tired?"

I nodded.

"You want to eat?"

I nodded.

"You like steak?"

I nodded.

"You like seafood?"

I nodded.

"All right. Let's go."

When we got in the truck, he said, "I need to change my clothes for dinner."

I looked down at my tight jeans, Nike tennis shoes. "What about me?"

"Yeah, I'll take you home to change."

"We can just eat somewhere regular . . ."

He didn't respond. I repeated, "We don't have to go anywhere special."

He emphasized. "I'm not a regular guy. If I do it, I do it big."

I rolled my eyes. He smiled at me. I stared out of the window. We rolled into a relatively modern town house community in Lancaster County. Rather impressed, I commented. "This is nice."

He opened the garage on an all-brick end unit. A covered car sat inside. Hip-hop graffiti was written all over the black walls in the garage.

I chuckled. "J-Rock, huh?"

He nodded. "Yep. That's me."

I walked with him through the narrow aisle in the garage. "So, is this your girlfriend's car?"

He looked over his shoulders and twisted his lips. "What do you think?"

I shrugged my shoulders. "I don't know."

He opened the door to the house and we stepped inside. He darted to the alarm pad. I walked in his direction. He hung his keys on a rack.

"I'm a single man."

"What?"

"I don't have a girlfriend. That's my car."

Relieved that he was at least available, I nodded. "Okay."

"I collect antique Benzes."

He motioned for me to follow. We walked upstairs into his huge kitchen. Black granite countertops. Chrome appliances. Hardwood floors. The living room was big and empty. A square birch wood table and four black chairs sat in the open space between the living room and kitchen. Black leather mats on the table. White walls decorated with large professionally framed posters. Run DMC. Big Daddy Kane. Eric B. & Rakim. Doug E. Fresh.

"Where did you get all these old-school posters?"

He poured water into a glass. "I collect them. You want something to drink?"

I shook my head. "You collect everything."

"I try to . . ."

A bluish gray, medium-sized Chinese Shar-pei sat quietly in his cage in the middle of the floor. I moaned, "Aw."

I knelt down by the cage. The dog looked in the other direction. I jiggled the door of his cage, "Hey, there."

John said, "That's my man, Rocky."

"Hi, Rocky."

"You like dogs, huh?"

"Yeah. He acts funny."

"He has to get used to you."

"Can I open the cage?"

He laughed. "He ain't gonna come out."

I opened the cage. Rocky moseyed out and sniffed my feet. I knelt down and patted his rough short coat. I wrapped my arm around his neck. He cuddled closely.

"You must be good people. Rocky don't deal with everybody."

I giggled. "I know how to communicate with dogs. Can I walk him?"

"I usually let him out back."

I pouted. "That's so mean. Let's walk him."

"All right."

As if this detour wasn't in his plans, he huffed and puffed while he put on Rocky's leash. When we stepped out of the front door, I expected Rocky to drag me along. Instead, he sluggishly sat on the first step. I turned to look at John. He laughed. "See, this could take all evening."

Finally, Rocky got up and strolled down the sidewalk. He walked at an elephant's pace. It was obvious this dog was deprived. I kidded John about his lazy dog. He shrugged his shoulders. "He's just the kind of dog I need."

I laughed. "Are you lazy?"

"No, I'm busy." He looked at his watch. "So, can we get back on schedule?"

I pouted and we walked back to the house. Rocky and I followed John upstairs. More and more posters greeted me. I felt like I was in the hip-hop Hall of Fame. When we got to the second floor, he pointed. "That's my room."

I peeped in the large room, but didn't get the message that he wanted to invite me in. He pointed to another room. "That's my son's room."

I nodded. He reminded me, "That's my little man."

"What's his name?"

He smiled. "John."

His sensitive expression made me blush. "Aw."

Following him, I walked up another flight of stairs into a loft. Furniture, finally. Rocky crawled under the large glass coffee table. PlayStation games and controls were tossed around the floor.

He grabbed a remote from the mini-bar. "This is where me and my boyz hang out."

Granting my approval, I nodded. "This is nice."

"Thanks."

He flicked on the large flat-screen plasma TV. Music boomed out of his surround sound. I covered my ears. He quickly turned the volume down.

"Sorry about that, sweetheart."

"It's okay."

He smiled at me. "Sit down."

I plopped down on the black leather sectional. He tossed the remote at me. "Here you go."

I looked at the complicated gadget and said, "Thanks."

He stood at the top steps. "I'll be ready in a few."

Rocky scooted closer to me and curled up by my feet. After deciphering the uses of the remote, I finally found HBO. *Meet the Parents* was on. I found myself giggling loudly.

At some point, I forgot that I wasn't alone. My eyes watered. I laughed hysterically. Then, in walks John and I'm totally embarrassed. I tucked my foot under me and leaned back on the couch, hoping to conceal my silliness.

"What's this?"

I mumbled. *Meet the Parents*.

He plopped down beside me. "This is my shit!"

Not what I'd expected of such a tough guy, but I didn't mind. He patted my knee. "We're gonna get along real well."

I blushed. "You think?"

He nodded. "I love a silly chick."

I poked my lips out. Slightly offended, my wrinkled forehead seemed to question that comment. He patted my knee to squash the insult. "I thought you were real deep. Don't get me wrong. I like deep chicks too, but I'm a simple guy. Sometimes I just like to relax and watch dumb ass movies and play PlayStation. Plus you're cool with Rocky. That's good shit."

For the first time all day, his dreamy eyes connected with mine. I lowered my chin. He lifted it with his index finger. "You feel me."

I nodded. "Good. We gotta get out of here. I made reservations for seven. You gotta get dressed."

He stood up, reached his hand out, and pulled me up. "I hope you don't take too long to get ready."

"Um . . . it doesn't take me long."

He laughed. "You don't sound too sure about that."

As I looked at his transformation, I wasn't. He wore a plaid Polo shirt, nice jeans, and black shoes, presumably Kenneth Cole. He was casual, but sharp. In my head, I visually shuffled through the clothes in my closet. Jeans. More jeans. T-shirts. More T-shirts. I wasn't prepared to go wherever he planned to take me. As I trotted down the two flights of stairs, I still couldn't visualize an outfit. He put Rocky in his cage. When we stepped out into the garage, I admitted, "I don't have anything to wear."

He ignored my first attempt. I tried again, "I mean. I only have jeans."

He clicked the car door opener. "You have those black shiny cargo pants."

Stunned by his accurate observation, I stopped. "What?"

He opened my door. "Girl, I told you I've been watching you for awhile."

As I climbed in, I looked at him suspiciously. "That's scary."

He laughed. "Oh. I'm not a stalker or nothing like that."

He closed the door and I wondered. What were his motives? I was scared, but interested. I was turned off, but intrigued. When he got in the car, he looked at me. "Why you look nervous?"

I shrugged my shoulders. "I'm not nervous."

He put the key in the ignition. "I didn't mean to scare you."

I nodded. He tried to reaffirm his sanity. "For real, I just like the way you look in those pants."

I forced the corners of my lips to curl. "Um-huh."

As the truck drifted out of the driveway, he slammed on brakes. He obviously sensed my doubt, and said, "You know where I live. You know my license tag number. You know where my studio is. I have too much to lose to be a stalker."

Feeling for him pity, I smiled. "You right."

He hit his fist into mine. "We cool?"

I nodded. "Yes, we're cool."

When we walked into my matchbox, I felt a little ashamed. He made himself immediately comfortable. He grabbed the TV remote. I opened my closet. Standing there with my hands on my hips, I felt wanted. David never took me to nice places for fear someone would recognize me. I was the beautiful doll to decorate his mantelpiece, but too delicate to be taken around. I sighed.

I pulled my cargo pants out. "Are these the ones?"

He nodded. "You know."

I pulled a white T-shirt out that had "Pisces" written in black metallic letters. I'd cut the collar from the shirt, so it fell off one shoulder. I grabbed a silver chain belt. I hustled around—underwear, deodorant, lotion, and tweezers. I dashed into the bathroom as if I was running from what was on the other side. I closed the door and leaned my back on it. Slowly, I slid down to a seated position. The reflection of me sinking warned me that I needed to get it together. As if I could control it, I gave myself instructions: *Stop trippin'. Breathe. Calm down.*

I laid my clothes on the toilet. I took deep breaths as I plucked my eyebrows. What if he just wants my body? What if he plans to do the same thing as Jordan? What if he doesn't even like me?

The water splashing in the tub settled the activity in my head. I inadvertently wet my hair. No way could I get the wild woolly look with the time constraint. I jumped out of the shower, stared in the mirror. A wet puppy looked back at me. The steam so dense, a blow-dryer was no option. I dried the mirror. With a rat-tail comb, I combed gel and mousse through my hair. I parted the middle and tucked the sides behind my ear. I twisted my lips. It had to do for the night. I decorated my eyes with dramatic silver shadow and silver liner. The sheer gloss always worked. I patted my lips together. Makeup has a mysterious way of covering the obvious. I felt pretty, whether it was real or not. I cracked the door for a little ventilation.

I heard John laughing. I smiled.

"Yo, it ain't like that. I'm just taking the girl out for a bite to eat."

I put my hand on my chest. I mouthed, "Just taking me out for a bite to eat."

I sighed. He laughed harder. Who was he talking to? Why hadn't he noticed I'd opened the door and turned the fan off?

I slipped on my clothes and sprayed Escada Hippie Cologne. I rummaged through my jewelry bag. My engraved heart pendant fell out. *Laila, You're My World.* I took a deep breath and clinched it to my chest. How he loved me. I hoped my heart could send apologetic waves to David. I let it rest there for a moment. Finally, I dropped it back in the bag and found my initial pendant. I clamped it on. The long script *L* hung right in my bony cleavage.

I swung the door open and walked out. "I'm ready."

As I struggled to slide my barefoot into my BCBG Mary Jane stilettos, I held onto the wall. I peeped up at John. His eyes were concentrated on the television. I stood outside the bathroom, my back turned to the mirror. I peered over my shoulder and rubbed my butt. Attempting to push my low-rise thong lower, I stuck my hand in my pants. From the corner of my eye, I could tell that John didn't as much as offer a semi-stimulated glance.

He stood up. "C'mon man."

He came closer. My stomach jolted. He helped me with my denim blazer. By the time I grabbed my purse, he already had the door open.

He took me to McCormick & Schmick's at the intersection of Market and Broad Street. Cars drove continuously around the traffic circle. Changes. Progression. I stared at the menu. The prices, I huffed. He grabbed my hand.

"Get whatever you want."

"Thank you."

"Don't trip. This is how I roll." He smiled, reached under the table and patted my leg. "This is how we roll."

He pushed my menu down to see my face. He smiled. "Pisces, huh?"

I nodded. "Yep."

He folded his hands on the table. "Romantic. Trusting. Forgiving." He snickered. "Naïve."

Why does that characteristic offend me so? I stretched my mouth open. "That's messed up."

"That's what they say. Right?"

I rolled my eyes. "That doesn't mean you have to repeat it."

He winked. "I was talking in general. Didn't mean to upset you." He leaned back in his chair. "You just had a birthday then."

I nodded. "Yep. March sixteenth."

"What did you do?"

I shook my head. "Absolutely nothing."

He frowned. "Why? Because you were new in town?"

I shrugged my shoulders. "Just 'cause."

As if he were solving a dilemma, he smiled. "We'll celebrate your birthday on April sixteenth."

Trying to pretend that it didn't faze me, I chuckled. "I don't feed into all the birthday hype. You know?"

Skepticism in his expression, he shook his head. "No."

I rolled my eyes. "I just don't get all excited about my birthday."

He shook his head. "I go all out for birthdays."

The manager came over and shook John's hand. "Hey, John. Good to see you."

John smiled. "Tony, this is Laila. She's a special lady."

Tony shook my hand. Then he patted John on the back. "Laila, this is a good man. One of my favorite customers."

John stated, "As much money as I spend in here, I should be your best customer."

They laughed. "Just let me know if you need anything. I'm sending a bottle of wine over, on the house."

When Tony walked away, John told me that he frequented the restaurant. I nodded. When the wine came, he made a toast. "To Laila. To me. To us."

Insinuation. Right? I blushed and swallowed my wine. The candle flickered between us. I saw my reflection in the window. I glowed.

After dinner, John dropped me off in front of my building. It was obvious that he wasn't going to offer as much as a hug, so I kissed his cheek before I jumped out. As I floated into the building, my legs were weightless. If the night was a dream, then I wanted to stay asleep.

CHAPTER 16

When I woke up, I called Danielle. Her voice made my excitement dwindle.

Before I could say anything, she said, "Hey, girl. Lemme call you back."

After a long pause, I sucked my teeth. "All right."

Hoping she would reconsider, I slowly slid the phone from my ear. When her receiver slammed down, I curled up in my bed and continued to dream.

Hours passed. Finally, Danielle returned my call. "Hey, Laila." Her voice was still rather melancholy. "Can I come over there?"

I sat up. "Yeah . . . what's up?"

"I'll tell you when I get there."

Danielle's normally tamed dreads were scattered on her head. Her three-year-old son stood beside her. The baby, Shandi, was clamped to her hip. A huge H&M bag hung from Danielle's forearm.

I reached out to hug her. "Hey, girl."

She forced a chuckle. "Girl."

As she limped into the apartment, she shook her head. "Laila, I'm tired."

She sat on the bed. Jacob climbed up on her free knee. Two babies clutched her bosom and she looked lost. As each tear rolled down, Jacob gently wiped them. Then, he kissed his mother. Why can't I have kids? A small amount of envy plagued me.

"What happened?"

"He said that if we're not going to be together, he's going to take Jacob."

I sighed. "You told him you wanted to leave?"

She nodded. I frowned. "Laila, I can't just disappear. He's their father."

That actually wasn't what I was saying. I ignored it and asked, "Do you think you can work on it?"

She shrugged her shoulders. The more Danielle and I talked, the more I realized that she instigated a lot of their arguments. Often, I even wondered if she intentionally ignited his jealous rage. For me, it seemed simple to do what I had to do to keep peace. Other people felt different. I tried to appear sympathetic. "Is it all about the whole trust issue?"

"He don't trust nobody, girl. I'm just tired of pretending. He wants me to be this quiet little, docile dummy. That ain't me."

I shrugged my shoulders. "Is that who you were when you met him?"

She rolled her neck and her eyes simultaneously. "No. I don't think so." As if my question frustrated her, she smacked her lips. "Whatever. That ain't me now."

I chuckled. Her eyes twitched. "He don't even know who I am."

"Whatchu mean?"

"I am so different around him. I don't talk. It's just messed up. I'm ready to be me." She took a deep breath. "I'm tired." Her eyes pleaded for my understanding. "You know?"

I nodded. "So whatchu gonna do?"

"I just want to move home with my mother and hopefully we can work out visitation and stuff."

"Do you think he's bluffin' about Jacob?"

She kissed his forehead and shook her head. Both Shandi

and Jacob were so disciplined, quietly snuggling with their needy mother. There was no way she could risk losing either of them.

She sniffed. "He's such a good father."

I didn't know what to say. My speechless moment was interrupted when my cell phone rang.

"Hello."

"What's up, homie?"

When I heard John's signature greeting, I was elated. "Hey, John."

In the midst of my girl's drama, I felt guilty for feeling so high. So, I concealed my intoxication and snuck into the bathroom. When I closed the door, I slid down to the floor and inhaled.

He asked, "Whatchu do all day?"

Ah! How could I explain that I did him all day? I lied. "Nothing much. What did you do?"

"Hung out at the studio."

My vocabulary escaped me, because all I said was, "Oh . . ."

He laughed at my weird response. "You tryna eat later?"

"Well, um . . ." I thought about Danielle. The kids. What was the right thing to do in my situation? I sighed. "My girl came over to visit and I . . ."

As I battled with the appropriate thing to do, he interrupted me. "Well, we can all go out . . ."

"She has her kids . . ."

As if kids wouldn't hinder our outing, he said, "How many?"

"Two. They're three and eighteen months."

He gasped. "They're young."

I rolled my eyes in my head. Shit! I wanted to leave her and her damn kids. Instead, I agreed. "Yeah, they are really young."

"Look, how about I grab something to go and bring it over?"

Resisting the urge to jump for joy, I calmly said, "Okay."

When I came out of the bathroom, Danielle looked suspicious. Trying to fight the flattery, I curled my lips. "Girl, that was mystery man."

She yelled, "Stop playin'! How many times have you talked to him?"

She snapped out of her own situation. I downplayed mine. "We hung out yesterday."

She bounced on the bed. "Tell me everything!"

Her eyes wandered into an unknown place as I told her about John. "Laila, it's so good when someone treats you like a lady."

"But he sends me mixed messages. He treats me like a home-girl or something."

She sat dazed. "He likes you. I know he does."

Trying to drift into the vision that she saw, I nodded. "I hope."

John popped up with carryout from Bluzette, my new favorite restaurant, and McDonald's Happy Meals for the kids. Hoping for a hug, I cracked the door so we would need to collide for him to get in. He pushed the door wider and patted the top of my head like he would a younger sister. When I turned around, I winked at Danielle. She smirked.

He made himself at home. After taking off his lightweight Polo jacket, he stepped in the bathroom to wash his hands. When he came out, he distributed the food as if we were visiting him. During dinner, we made small talk and John got acquainted with the kids. "Li'l man, you gonna eat those fries?"

He teased Jacob by raising the fries up and down. Then, he'd give them to him. He appeared to enjoy the cat and mouse game more than Jacob. Just as Jacob would get frustrated, he'd hand him the fry.

Once finished eating, Danielle dominated the conversation with her drama. Smoke seemed to puff out of John's ears as she insinuated that her boyfriend was abusive. He cringed and rubbed Shandi's hair. "How could he put you through all of that, after you pushed these beautiful kids out?"

He added, "My baby's mother is everything to me."

Danielle and I sneered at each other. She asked what I wanted to know. "Are y'all still together?"

He snickered. "No."

We nodded. Danielle asked, "Why?"

"I did some things." He smirked. "She did some things." With a dreadful expression on his face, he continued. "We stopped trusting each other. I refused to have my son see us on a roller coaster. So, we agreed to let it go." He shrugged his shoulders. "It was our decision, both of us. No trust, no relationship. Outside of being in an intimate relationship, I trust her with my life. She's my best friend. I love her to death."

I took a deep breath. Could I really deal with a man with so much love for the mother of his child? The room got silent. Jacob running in circles around the six hundred square feet of space and screaming destroyed the pressure to speak. We chatted about trivial topics, but it was obvious we could not talk about relationships.

Before John left, he asked Danielle, "Are you staying here tonight?"

She looked at me and shrugged her shoulders. I smiled, "You can if you want . . ."

She nodded. John chuckled. "It's a little snug up in here. Do want to stay at a hotel?"

We both looked confused. She shook her head. "I don't have money to stay at a hotel."

"That's not what I asked you." He repeated. "Do you want to stay at a hotel?"

She shrugged her shoulders. "I guess."

He reached in his pocket and peeled off three one-hundred-dollar bills. He walked over to Danielle. She didn't reach her hand out. He dropped it in her lap. "Those kids don't deserve to be cramped up in here. This should take care of two nights. Lemme know if you need anything."

She sat as if the money on her lap was a bomb. Before John turned to face me, my eyes directed her to show some sign of gratitude. Her stunned expression made him smile. I guess he knew what she wanted to say. Finally, she jumped up and hugged him. "Oh my God! Thank you so much."

"Ain't nothing, homie."

He walked over and pounded my fist. "All right, homie. I'll hit you tomorrow."

I followed him to the door. No kiss. No hug. He patted my head and shut the door behind him.

I turned around to see Danielle jumping up and down. "Oh my God! Laila, he is so sweet!"

I nodded. "I know, but I don't think he likes me like that."

She pushed me. "Girl, you better wake up and smell the coffee. He don't seem like the type of dude that wastes time on chicks. He has to like you." She waved her bills in the air like we had just hit the jackpot. "He looked out for your girl that he just met like this."

I shrugged my shoulders. "I think he just likes to toss his money around, but he doesn't give me the vibe that he really likes me."

"You better make him."

CHAPTER 17

Ann yelled to the back of the office. "Laila. C'mere." As I strolled to the front, she yelled again. "Hurry up."

Her raspy voice forced me to walk slower. When I got halfway down the hall, I noticed flowers. She was walking toward me. I smiled. "Who sent those to you?"

She cackled. "You gotta sign for 'em. They're for you."

For me? My heart dropped. What if David knew where I worked? I stopped in my tracks. My eyes shifted from side to side. I said, "Hand me the card first."

She huffed. The delivery guy shook his head. She pushed the flowers toward me. As if I didn't want them to touch me, I yanked my neck back and snatched the card out. *Happy Birthday, Homie.*

Happy birthday? I mouthed. "What?"

I looked at the calendar on Ann's desk and shook my head. That crazy John was really celebrating my birthday on April six-teenth. The delivery guy looked surprised. With my hand over my mouth, I rushed to him. "I'm so sorry." Trying to explain, I said, "I don't accept gifts from strangers. So I just wanted to make sure I knew who sent them."

As if I could save the explanation, he handed me a pen and

didn't comment. Before I could even finish signing, Ann looked at me. "So, who's the lucky guy?"

Trying hard not to blush, I shook my head. "Just a guy."

She folded her arms. "What guy? What's his name?"

I rolled my eyes. She stretched hers open. I waved my hand. "No one. Seriously."

"You're telling me no one sent you orchids?"

I nodded. She grunted. "Well he must have some class. Only men with class send orchids."

As she attempted to pry his name out of me, I smirked.

"Girl, you'll go to your grave with a secret."

I shrugged my shoulders. "It's not a secret. It's just not that serious."

"Laila, you're something else."

I laughed and headed into Jordan's old office. Before I dialed John's number, I sat there baffled. His actions didn't show that he wanted more. He still called me "Homie." A peck on the cheek was the max of his affection. Why the hell send flowers?

When I called, he picked up with the same greeting, "What's up, homie?"

I sighed. "Thanks for the flowers."

"Why do you sound so sad?"

"I don't know . . . I just . . . Never mind."

I tucked in my bottom lip and stared into space.

"What's wrong?"

As if he could see, I shook my head. Now agitated, he growled. "What's wrong?"

"Nothing, John. I'm fine."

Still with a tinge of irritation, he asked, "You wanna hook up later?"

After five lavish dinners in three weeks and no signs of affection, I wasn't sure if he was worth wasting my time on. And damn if I wanted to hear anything else about his baby's mama. I sighed. "I don't know."

He coaxed. "C'mon. I made reservations."

What would it hurt? It's not like someone else was offering to take me to dinner. Without any more convincing, I surrendered.

Just minutes before John's expected arrival, I sat in my apartment, snacking on Peanut Chews. Why take an hour to get really glamorous when he doesn't even notice? I didn't bother to redo the five French braids that I had lazily put in my hair the night before. With the subtle gloss and eyeliner look, I walked out to his truck around eight o'clock.

When I got in the car, he handed me a card. There was a hand-drawn picture of a slim, black lady with angelic wings. Her eyes were closed. Her eyelashes were practically an inch long. She stood in front of a microphone. I opened the card.

You were born with wings. So fly.
Happy Birthday, Angel.
Your homie, John.

I stared at the card. After digesting his words, I looked at him. "Did you draw this?"

He smirked. "Whatchu think?"

I smiled. "I don't know."

He shook his head. I laughed. "What?"

"Who else would draw it?'

"I don't know."

"Who do you think painted the studio? My garage? The pictures in my house?"

I shrugged my shoulders. He shook his head. "I thought I told you that art was my second love."

"I don't remember."

He put his hand on top of mine. "You don't know me."

Sarcastically, I asked, "And whose fault is that?"

He pushed my hand away. "Who else's?"

I raised my eyebrows. He shook his head. "Girl, you're a trip."

We laughed. As always, the music blasted and prevented us

from deepening our connection. I watched how peaceful he seemed. Nothing seemed urgent. As much as I told myself that I didn't want him, I did. Was I afraid? Shit, was he afraid? And more important, how could I handle him and his damn baby's mama?

As we ate, I asked my heart questions. I negotiated with my brain. What should I do with this man?

When we finished eating, I ordered another drink. As we waited, the table was cleared. There was nothing left for me to concentrate on, except him. He gazed into my eyes. My nerves shuddered. My eyes flickered. He grabbed both of my hands.

"What's up with the barrier?"

Disappointed in his question, I looked down. "What?"

"Why is it so hard to connect with you?"

I opened my mouth and began to say what I couldn't explain. So, my mouth hung open. Speechless. Then, I bit my lip to avoid saying the wrong thing. What was I doing to make people say this about me? Why did everyone feel that I had a wall around me?

"You seem so cold."

Questioning the image I portray, I shrugged my shoulders. "But I'm not."

"It's like every time I try, you put up this electric fence."

My mouth twisted from side to side. "Whatever."

I smiled. He didn't. "It's like you're afraid to let someone in."

My heart screamed for love. Why couldn't anyone see that? Were my actions unconsciously protecting my heart from destruction? I nodded. "I am."

He smiled. "Don't be."

"Why?"

He tightened his grip on my hands. His eyes concentrated on my eyes. His voice stretched out and captivated my heart. "Because I'm here. I'm ready to be what you need."

He paused and flipped my hands over. He rubbed the balls of his thumbs in my palms. "Stop fighting. I want to protect you."

Positioned in a defenseless state, I absorbed his words. Was he trying to say that we could cut out the friend shit? All I could think to say was, "Really?"

We laughed and he confirmed, "Really."

We sat still. He smiled at me. I smiled at him. Frozen in the moment. Finally, I leaned up and licked my lips. "Why don't you ever touch me?"

"Cause I don't get that vibe from you."

"So what do I need to do for you to get that vibe?"

He blushed, as if he was embarrassed. "You don't have to do anything. I just didn't want to force you to do anything you weren't ready for."

My mind would have said something innocent, but my body blurted out, "Oh, I'm ready."

As if he had awaited this moment, he looked as if he were ready to skip out of the restaurant. "Really?"

His schoolboy excitement made me giggle. "Yes, really."

He let my hands go and he grabbed his wallet. He put the money in the folder and stood up from the table in a matter of seconds. He wanted it as much as I. And I anxiously followed. As we headed to his car, he transformed into an over-affectionate man. Touching. Stroking. Caressing. Every gesture aroused me.

When he opened the passenger door, he pushed me against the truck and tasted my lips. His scent, his leaning close to me made me shiver. My inhibitions began to fade away. I mumbled, "C'mon. Let's go."

He nibbled on my ear. "There's no rush."

Maybe not for him, but I was horny. Still, he obliged as he rushed around to the driver's side. When he hopped in the truck, our eyes connected. It was our night and we both knew it. Steam seemed to rise between us as he put the key in the ignition. He turned me on. My hips twitched in my seat to calm the tremor in my panties. As he pulled out of his parking space, I reached over to caress his leg. As I stroked the bulge in his jeans, he drove recklessly. The speed, the wind, him filling to capacity all made me high.

When we pulled up into his driveway, I could not take the anticipation, so, I gripped it tightly. He looked at me. I stared down at the rock in my palm. Without questioning my impatience, he kissed me. He tangled his fingers in two of my cornrows.

When we momentarily took a breath, he moaned. "C'mon. Let's go into the house."

With passion so intense, I ignored his request. He breathed me. I inhaled him. He slid his chair back. I pulled my skirt up around my waist and straddled him. The horn beeped. It startled us. With our lips pasted together, we chuckled. He rubbed my bare bottom. He yanked my thong to the side. I humped. He tantalized my escalation point. I held his face in my hands to look into the eyes of the man that quenched my thirst with just his fingers. My cloud drizzled on him. He reached up my shirt and massaged my breasts. I unbuckled his pants.

He begged. "Let's go inside."

I ignored his request once more. He struggled to pull his jeans below his waist. He fumbled to get the rubber from his wallet. I grabbed the rubber and ripped the paper open. I rolled it onto him. I twirled on him and moistened his grass. It tickled. I moaned and anxiously lifted my body to grant him access to my dome. He conceded. My eyes fluttered. Zero resistance. Complete reception. He fit like pantyhose. He applied unrelenting pressure. He twiddled my nipples. I pounded on him. The night air entered through the windows. Loud panting escaped through the sunroof. Aggression in his roar, expectation in my moan, we met in the middle somewhere between triumph and redemption.

We sat quietly, clasped together. He kissed me softly. "C'mon. Can we go inside now?"

I chuckled and nodded. He opened the door. I climbed off him and hopped out, adjusting my skirt. He pulled his jeans up and sloppily buckled his belt.

He joked. "I know my neighbors heard you screaming."

I batted my eyes. "I'm sorry."

We walked into the garage. "You shocked me."

"Why?"

"I just didn't expect you to be like that."

We walked upstairs. Rocky stood inquisitively in his cage, as if to ask why it took us so long from the time he heard the garage door open. I giggled. "Hey, Rocky. Were you looking for Daddy?"

The dog paced from side to side. I unlatched the cage. He sat there with an attitude. We laughed. "He must smell sex on us."

John walked over and put a cookie up to my mouth. "Here you go, baby."

After I bit the cookie, he kissed me. He licked the crumbs from my mouth. Rocky growled. We giggled.

"C'mon. Let's go upstairs."

After three visits, I finally walked into his bedroom for the first time. "I don't have anything to sleep in."

He curled his lips. "We ain't sleeping tonight."

I rolled my eyes. "You know what I mean."

He pulled me to him. "I don't want you to sleep in anything."

He slid his hand up my skirt and pulled down my soaked panties. I helped. Skirt down. Top off. I leaned on the high bed-post. I swayed from side to side. He dropped to his knees and kissed my stomach. Then, he kissed my inner thigh. My legs weakened. While I moved to sit on the edge of the bed, he pulled his shirt up and ripped his jeans off. I scooted back horizontally on the bed and spread like an eagle. He rubbed his palm over my crystal ball like a psychic. As if the fortune was suitable, he kissed it. He loved it. And he brought joy to our future.

CHAPTER 18

I woke to hear the dog whining at the foot of the bed. Initially, I was confused about where I was. I rubbed my eyes, trying to refocus my vision. John swung his arm over me. "You all right?"

"Um-huh."

He rubbed my stomach. I moaned. Having a man beside me early in the morning felt like heaven. I rolled over on my side to face him. I propped my head up with my hand. I stroked his six o'clock shadow. "Good morning."

He nodded.

"I have to be at work by twelve."

"What time is it?"

I peeped at the clock. "Seven forty-five."

He chuckled. "I'll get you home in time."

His eyes remained closed. I stared at his handsome face and got turned on again. I fiddled with his earring. I leaned in and nibbled his earlobe. He cleared his throat. "You wore me out last night."

"Whatever. You're the one who was acting like the Energizer Bunny."

He crawled out of bed. Nothing covered his ripped body. I got up and scrounged around for my clothing. I found everything except my panties. I knelt to look under the bed. Though the bed stood really high, the frame was literally five inches from the floor. My panties sat peacefully alone, far from the edge. I lay flat and reached my hand under the bed to no avail. When John came back in the room, he looked down at me struggling.

"Don't kneel over like that. I can't handle it."

"I'm trying to get my . . ."

He grabbed a twisted wire hanger from his dresser. "Here. Use this."

After I had successfully retrieved my panties, I asked, "Do you have some sweats that I can wear?"

He looked in his drawer and handed me a pair of sweatpants and a T-shirt. I showered and washed my half-braided hair. I threw on the sweats and the Nike slippers that he had given me. When I was dressed, I went downstairs to get Rocky's walking leash.

I called for the dog. John called downstairs. "Hold up. Wait for me."

Morning mist, mixed with the smell of fresh greenery, graced the air as we strolled through the development. Our relationship felt more complete, compared to the quickie I experienced with Jordan.

Just as I felt content with discarding my armor, it dawned on me that this was only the morning after. We hadn't been through one good week of sex. That will decide how far this goes. Men never act funny the first day. Suddenly, I withdrew. What if it was all a part of the grand scheme? I released his hand and folded my arms. Rocky stopped to do his business. I stared off into the fog.

"What's wrong?"

I shrugged my shoulders. "Nothing. Why?"

I shook my head and we continued to walk. Was it too soon to question what he wanted from me? I decided to keep my feelings to myself. No need to end it before it had begun.

*   *   *

When I walked into the office, Ann commented that I glowed. I smirked.

"I guess your smile has to do with those flowers you got yesterday."

I shook my head. "No. I'm just in a good mood."

I didn't need caffeine. I was still high from John's touch, his smell.

As the hours flew by, my intoxication slowly evaporated. Why didn't he call? The phone rang. I practically yanked it from Ann. "Ryder's Chiropractic. Laila speaking."

"Girl, I called you all night," said Danielle.

I put her on hold and rushed into the spare office. Since Danielle was the main promoter of my relationship with John, I anxiously gave her a play by play description of my seduction.

"Did you work 'em, girl?"

As if I was convinced, when I really wasn't, I bragged, "I sure did."

"So, now do you think he likes you?"

"I don't know. I haven't talked to him since this morning."

"You better call him. You know he's going to be at the club tonight."

I giggled. "Yeah. I know."

"Do you need me to pick you up or do you think he will?"

"I don't know. I'll call you and let you know. How are things with Ray?"

"He's been cool for a few days. We're just trying to work it out. You know?"

I shook my head, thankful that at least I was out of that cycle. "Yeah. I know."

By the time I walked into my apartment, John still hadn't called. I contemplated calling him, but . . .

The phone rang. "Hey, baby."

A smile stretched across my face. Baby, not homie. "Hey."

He chuckled. "So, I guess you came over, fucked my brains out and weren't going to call."

I laughed. "John. Stop playin'. Why didn't you call me?"

"I was in the studio all day. I had a lot of music in my head after last night."

My high was slowly creeping back. "Really?"

"Yeah. I put down some bangin' beats today."

"That's good." I hesitated, but then I admitted, "I wrote today."

"You gon' read it tonight?"

"Not at the club, but . . ."

"At our after-party."

I giggled, "Yes."

"You rollin' with me?"

"Of course."

"I'll be there at eight."

I relaxed in the tub for about thirty minutes. The soulful sound of Vivian Green blessed my meditation. I blew out my hair and flipped it. I slipped on my tightest jeans so John could lust for me all evening.

When I hopped in his truck, he kissed me. "Hey, baby."

I joked. "Hey, homie."

"That homie shit is over . . ."

I rejoiced in the thought we were approaching a new level. When we got into the club, Danielle was near the bar. She came up to us. Her vivid excitement told that she knew of our sexual encounter. John laughed.

"I guess your girl knows we slept together last night?" said John.

"Why would you say that?"

He shook his head and pulled a chair out for me. "When you gonna be ready to record?"

I had almost forgotten about the initial goal. I shrugged my shoulders. "When you want me to?"

He ordered drinks. "Whenever you ready."

"Okay."

"Don't wait too long. I may have to scoop up another poet to take your place."

"What?"

He pushed my leg. "I'm just fucking with you. Fix your face."

I rolled my eyes. "So, is that your M.O.? You come and scoop up all the new talent in the club."

He leaned towards me and tugged my belt loops. "Laila, you don't even believe that shit yourself. How long did it take me to say something to you?"

I remarked. "Well don't play like that then."

He messed in my hair. "You don't have to trip. I told you. By the time I approach somebody, I already know what I want from them."

He provided the perfect segue to the questions lingering in my mind. "So, what do you want from me?"

Without hesitation, he stepped to the challenge. "I want you. I want to know everything about you. I want to be the man you describe in your poetry. The one who makes your struggle worthwhile."

Birds chirped in my ear, but fear filled my stone heart. How was I to open my heart again? I rubbed his head and pecked him. "Thank you."

His desires were similar to promises I had heard before. I prayed John was different.

As if my expression told him that I was dissatisfied with his offer, he asked, "What do you want from me?"

I paused. I wasn't prepared. "I want you to stay the way you are," I sighed. "I want friendship. I want love. I want honesty."

He shook my hand. "You got that."

Sincerity seeped through the palm of his hand. The words to Vivian Green's song, tiptoed through my head. "Is it too much to ask?"

CHAPTER 19

For four weeks, the first thing I saw when I opened my eyes was John resting beside me. Many of my clothes were in his closet.

One morning I rolled over to find him sitting on the edge of the bed using his cell phone. I rubbed his back. His voice disturbed me. He repeated, "C'mon now."

I scooted closer and put my arms around his waist. He acknowledged my presence by patting my head. A female's voice hollered through the phone. My heart thumped.

"Keisha, calm down and listen!"

I took a deep breath, because I had yet to experience Baby Mama Drama. It sounded like it was on the other end. I tugged at my bottom lip.

"I haven't introduced you to her yet, because . . ."

I got out of the bed and walked into the bathroom to give him privacy. When I returned, he was holding the cell phone in his hand with his head hung low. I walked over to him and hugged him.

"What's up?"

He grunted. "You ready to meet my son's mother?"

"Huh?"

He shrugged his shoulders. "That's how we do. We agreed that if and when we get serious, we would introduce the person."

"I don't know. Don't you think that's awkward?"

"Baby, my son hasn't spent a night with me in four weeks. I owe my little man more than that."

"But you still see him every day, right?"

"That's not enough for me." He paused. "I think I'm sure about you now. I got a feeling you gonna be around for a while, so it's time for y'all to meet."

I kissed his forehead. "I do plan to be around." I plopped down on the bed. "So, when are we meeting?"

"In a minute."

Feeling off guard, I shouted, "Where?"

He gestured for me to calm down. He smiled at me. "IHOP on City Line."

"Is she bringing JJ?"

He shook his head. It made me nervous that I was about to meet the only woman he ever loved. I mumbled, "What time?"

"In an hour."

We walked into the restaurant. He dialed Keisha. "Yeah, we're already here."

He looked out the window while he talked. She was obviously in the parking lot. My nerves percolated. She walked in. Her long locks were pulled up in a ponytail. She was all of four foot, eleven. Her glowing bronze complexion complimented the gold highlights. Although petite, her wide hips were stuffed in a pair of stretch jeans. She gave me the once over and forced a smile. John touched her shoulder and mine.

"Keisha, this is my girl, Laila. Laila, this is my son's mother, Keisha."

We shook hands and sang, "Nice to meet you."

"Jay, did you already get a table?"

She whined his name as if she owned him. I felt like an intruder. John tilted his head and looked at her. She pushed his arm and laughed. "Jay, you're silly."

I was so irritated by her voice, the way she called my man's name. Ugh!

The waiter said, "Wright. Party of three."

John went first. We followed, like two faithful wives. She thought she was Mrs. Wright and I wanted to be Mrs. Wright. It just wasn't right. It was awkward and eerie.

When we got to the table, I scooted into a booth. John sat across from me. Keisha slid in beside her baby's daddy. It was as if I were being interviewed. John looked over the menu. She put her hand on his menu. "Jay, what are you getting?" Before he answered, she said, "The regular?"

He laughed. "You know it."

The waiter came to take our drink order and Keisha spoke for the whole table. "We're ready."

No one asked if I was ready, but I shook the irritation and ordered a short stack of pancakes. Keisha ordered for both her and John. "We'll have the garden omelet."

As Keisha looked to me for a reaction, I took a deep breath and tried to appear calm. When the waiter walked away, she said, "So I finally meet Laila."

Her infliction was as if she were agitated by the thought of John seeing someone. I nodded.

"Where are you from again?"

"South Florida."

"Why Philly of all places?"

I shrugged my shoulders. "I got a job here."

"What do you do?"

I huffed. John laughed. "Damn, Keisha."

She laughed. "I'm sorry."

She hit his arm. "You're so silly, Jay."

If she called his name like that one more time, I was going to scream. The introduction was merely to let me know who was in charge. She moved on from questioning me to talking about JJ.

They giggled uncontrollably as they swapped stories about their seed. When the awkwardness became a little unbearable, I wandered to the bathroom. I paced back and forth. Why did they ever break up? He looked just as happy to be around her as she did with him. Could I condemn him for his honesty? Was this the way for him to have the best of both worlds?

The door swung open. Keisha's face startled me. I jumped. "Hey!"

She went into the stall. "Laila, why have you been in here so long?"

I started walking to the door. "I'm leaving now."

"Wait for me."

Reluctantly, I did. She came out, buttoning her jeans. She washed her hands, turned around and leaned against the sink.

"Laila, do you have kids?"

I shook my head.

"Do you know why I wanted to meet you?"

I shrugged my shoulders. "Not really."

She sighed. "Well, it's obvious that John cares about you. And JJ means the world to both of us." She paused. "I feel more comfortable knowing who my son is going to be around."

"I understand."

"Most women can't handle our relationship."

I smirked. She smiled. "Trust me. We're just really close. We spent a lot of years together. Nothing means more to me than his happiness and I think he feels the same about me."

I wanted to understand and maybe it was too mature for me to relate, but I was not ready. "The only reason I came in here after you was to reassure you. John tells me everything and I know how he feels about you. If you were some chick I thought would be gone tomorrow, I wouldn't have even bothered, but I know he wants to be with you and I respect that."

My impression of her slowly transformed. How many women would go so far to reassure the other woman? I hugged her. "Keisha, I admire you. You're a helluva woman."

She ignored the compliment. "I have a helluva baby daddy and he deserves to be happy."

Amazed at her strength, I looked at her and hugged her again.

"I like to be around whenever JJ meets someone new."

I nodded. "I understand."

"I wouldn't want him to feel uncomfortable getting to know you. If we're both there, he warms up sooner." She smiled. "So, when do you want to meet our li'l man?"

"Whenever . . ."

"I'll talk to Jay. Maybe I'll bring him by later."

Isn't it ironic how some people go overboard for the happiness of their child and others simply don't care? I hugged her one last time.

We walked back to the table. John chatted on the phone. The tension was gone and John noticed. He smiled. "I thought y'all rolled out."

Keisha punched his shoulder. "Shut up."

Maybe there was no need to question John. If Keisha still possessed so much love and respect for him, maybe he was a good man. The meeting validated our relationship for me.

When Keisha came over with JJ, I was in the kitchen making a peanut butter and jelly sandwich. She rang the doorbell. John stayed upstairs, playing PlayStation. My head pounded.

I opened the door. Keisha was tilted over with JJ on her hip. He was about three-fourths her size. She hobbled in the house.

"Hi, Laila."

The awkwardness resurfaced. "Hi, Keisha."

She put JJ down. "Li'l man, say hi to Ms. Laila."

He hugged her knee. She tapped the back of his head. "Say hi, boy."

I bent down. "Hi, John."

He smiled and tucked his head between his mother's legs. She dragged him along and sat at the table. He put his head on her lap and peeped at me.

"Where's Jay?"

I cringed, but shook the feeling with a smile. "He's upstairs."

She pushed JJ. "Go get Daddy."

I yelled upstairs. "John."

JJ came over to the steps and repeated. "John."

We laughed. He called him again. We laughed harder. John came tramping down the steps. He scooped him up and swung him around. "Boy, what's my name?"

He giggled. "John."

John put his fist in JJ's chest. "What?"

"John!"

He jacked his shirt up. "Whatchu say?"

I got my sandwich from the kitchen and sat at the table with Keisha. We both watched in admiration as the father and son wrestled.

Finally, after several attempts, JJ surrendered. "Sike. Sike." He laughed hysterically. "Daddy. Daddy."

John shook his hand. "That's my man."

Keisha said, "Jay, tell him to speak to Laila."

John said, "Say hi."

He mumbled. "Hi, Laila."

"Aw . . ." His sweet voice made my heart flutter. "Hi, John."

"My name JJ. John Isaiah Wright, Jr."

We all laughed. He ran in circles. He screamed. "My name JJ!"

As if he knew that he was the light in the dim house, he danced. He sang. He teased the poor dog. We sat around like one big happy family. I began to appreciate the love in the room. As he performed for us, I wondered if he'd ever understand the sacrifice his parents made. I slightly envied the adoration in the eyes of proud parents, gazing at their happy child. Keisha owned a part of John that I would probably never have the privilege to share.

Keisha stood up, "I see everything's cool here. I'm about to go."

"Where you going?"

She winked at me. "On a date."

She giggled. I smiled. John asked, "With who?"

"That guy I told you about . . ."

"Which one?

"The one I don't really like."

"Why you going then?"

Their debate forced the uncertainty to resurface. My eyes shifted back and forth. She put him on pause with her hand. "Because I can."

She bent down and kissed JJ. "See you later, baby."

He grabbed her neck tightly. "Bye, Mommy."

How could someone sacrifice the opportunity to hear that word? She stumbled as she pulled away from JJ. She pounded John's fist. "A'ight, homie."

He patted her head. "Have fun."

She left the house. John looked at me. I shrugged my shoulders. He lifted his son up on his neck. JJ beat his head like a drum. I laughed. "I guess we're in for the night."

He nodded and walked over to me. He bent down and kissed me. JJ whined, "I wanna kiss."

John held his legs tightly as JJ stamped his seal of approval on me. He slobbered on my lips, but it felt like no other kiss before.

As it got later, it was obvious JJ yearned for a mother's touch. He climbed up on me while we watched cartoons. He tucked his head into my chest. The heat from his body warmed me. I rubbed his delicate face. He mumbled. "I want juice."

I scooted up. John interrupted our bonding moment. "Give him water."

He pouted. "I don't want water." He demanded. "I want juice."

John snapped. "Boy, what did I say?"

JJ poked his lips out. I tipped him onto his feet, grabbed his hand, and swung my legs off the bed. We walked down the stairs, one footstep at a time.

When we got into the kitchen, I grabbed a kid's cup from the cabinet. JJ looked at me. He batted his big brown eyes and low-ered his head. "Can I have juice?"

His innocence stole my heart, but I didn't want to go against his father's wishes. I tucked the cup under the water spout. "Baby, your daddy said to give you water."

He whined. "Please, Mommy. I mean, Lay-Lay."

He created his own nickname for me. I blushed. He could have whatever he wanted. I was sold. With my finger over my mouth, I whispered, "Shh . . ."

I got another cup and poured him a little orange juice. He smiled. We stood in the kitchen while he swallowed his juice. Then, we walked upstairs with the water, as if we'd followed the rules.

When we got in the room, John smiled. "I know he worked you."

"Whatchu mean?"

"He's a player. I know he got some juice out of you."

I felt played, but it was worth it. I sat him up on the bed and kissed his cheek. "He can play me whenever he wants."

As if he understood, he jolted his head up and down. He gig-gled. I smiled. John seemed impressed.

CHAPTER 20

When we woke up, JJ sat quietly in his room watching cartoons. I tiptoed into his room. "Hey, li'l man."

He smiled. I asked, "You wanna eat?"

He whined, "Yes."

I reached out for his hand. "C'mon."

"Whatchu wanna eat?"

He smiled. "Cookies."

John heard us in the hallway. "Don't give that boy cookies this morning."

This little boy could take all my money. I sucked my teeth. "I'm not crazy enough to give him cookies this early in the morning."

He stumbled around the room. "I keep trying to tell you that boy is a player. He'll work you if you let him."

I ignored him.

The cabinets seemed bare. Finally, we agreed on something. He nodded when I pulled out the Strawberry Frosted pop tarts. I slightly got excited myself. I laid the pop tarts on a paper towel. He pointed to the toaster. "Put 'em in there."

I tried to reason with the toddler. "They taste better in here."

He yelled. "No. In there."

I popped his in the toaster and put mine in the microwave. I poured two glasses of milk and set them on the table. We sat together.

He watched me dunk my pop tart into my milk. With a mischievous grin, he followed. Back and forth we went; him, then me. I giggled like I was in pre-school.

The doorbell rang and ended our little celebration. His biological mother had come. I rushed to the door, John hot on my heels. I turned around, irritated by his anxiousness. I paused. "Do you want to get the door or do you want me to get it?"

"You can get it."

I opened the door. Keisha moseyed in wearing last evening's outfit. Of course, John noticed.

"Looks like you had fun last night."

She ignored the comment as she bent to catch her excited son as he ran to her. He yelled, "Mommy!"

She hugged him. "Hey, baby."

She kissed him over and over. "I missed you."

As if he was afraid of being disloyal, he peeped at me before responding. "I missed you too."

She picked him up. He leaned on her shoulder. She headed for the steps. "C'mon baby. Let's get your stuff."

She and JJ walked up the stairs. Keisha was the woman of the house. I tried to ignore my insecurities. John hugged me. "You cool?"

I nodded.

"You've passed the first test. It's time for you to meet my mother."

When he talked about his mother, he seemed to glorify her. I queried, "Are you sure you want me to meet your mother so soon?"

He nodded. "Yep. She's cooking dinner for us today."

Keisha came down the steps. She chimed in, "Your mother's cooking today?"

"Yep."

"I might stop by there."

I smiled tightly. Why did she want to hang around so much? She was obviously quite comfortable with the situation at hand. It drove me crazy.

John's mother turned out to be quite a sweetheart. She was naturally loving and maternal. When we walked in, she hugged me.

"Hello, young lady."

I smiled. "Hello."

She smiled at John. "She's more beautiful than you described."

She filled our plates and sat across the table from us. Her mixed gray bun sat lopsided on her head. I tried to ignore it, but kept noticing it. She didn't ask any questions about my past. She was solely interested in how happy I made her son. Before we left, she offered me her phone number. "Call me anytime."

Her gesture made me feel special. I was delighted that Keisha decided not to come. It made the visit all the more relaxed. When we got in the truck, John sighed.

"You need a car."

I raised my eyebrows. He laughed. "Not like that, baby."

I smirked.

"It's just those days you gotta be to work at nine that kill me."

"You want me to go home?"

He frowned. "Nah, never that. I wish you could stay every night."

I smiled. He nodded. "I'm gonna see what we can do about getting you a ride."

I huffed. "John, I don't want you to get me a ride. I'm saving my money. I'll get something soon."

He grabbed my hand. "You're my girl now. I'm going to get you a ride."

I pleaded. "I really don't . . ."

"If it makes you feel better, give me the money you saved up and it will be like you helped me get a ride."

Too embarrassed to admit that I hadn't saved a dime, I pouted. "Nope. I don't want you to help me. I'll do it myself."

He looked in my eyes. "You're my girl, right?"

I nodded.

"Then, let me be your man."

The struggle for my independence seemed like a losing battle. I smiled. "I'll try."

CHAPTER 21

Three months into the relationship, I finally decided to surrender. Why doubt him before he gave me reason? He was my man and he wanted to love me. Though it was hard to believe, I decided to enjoy the fantasy for as long as it lasted.

I stood in the mirror waiting for my man. The phone rang. I grabbed my keys and answered when I got in the hallway. "Hey, baby. I'm on my way out of the building."

I hung up before he responded. Each time I looked into his eyes, I experienced this rush. I dashed out of the door for yet another night with him. I looked left. I looked right. I pulled out my cell phone and began to dial his number. A horn blew.

My phone rang. "Baby, I'm right across the street."

He opened the door to a two-door navy blue Honda Accord. He stood up and smiled. I strutted across the street. "Where's your truck?"

"At the house."

Hesitantly, I nodded. "Okay."

He dangled the keys at me. "Here you go, baby."

Afraid that he was offering me the car as a gift, I pretended to be confused. "What?"

He smirked and shook his head. "Just a little something I picked up from the auction."

"That's nice."

"Why don't you drive tonight?"

I hesitated. He placed his hand on my shoulder. "Laila, this is your car. I bought it for you."

I forced a smile then hugged him. "Thanks, but I thought I told you that . . ."

He covered my mouth. "You gotta learn how to accept gifts. That's the kinda man I am."

I nodded. He asked, "Do you want to drive?"

Half-blushing, I grabbed the keys. "Yeah, I'll drive."

I hadn't as much as started a car since I arrived in Philly. After I adjusted the mirrors and the seat, I just sat there. I readjusted mirrors. I readjusted the seat. Finally, I took a deep breath and pulled off.

When we stopped at the first light, John reached over and cupped my breast. I giggled. "Stop. I have to concentrate."

He put his hand up my shirt. "I like this."

I tapped his hand. "Stop."

We laughed. He pulled away. "Okay, I'm sorry. I just can't keep my hands off you."

"Um-huh."

When we got out of the car, I reminded him, "I don't believe you got this car, when I told you . . ."

"Okay, let's put it like this. It's my car. You can just borrow it whenever you want."

It seemed reasonable. I smiled at him. "I love you."

The words seemed to slip out so freely. I took my hands off him. Shit! I couldn't believe what I'd just said. He turned around and put his arm around my shoulder. "I love you too, Laila."

As we walked into the club, I snuggled close to him. Danielle was in her usual spot. I walked over to her. "I did it."

Anxiously, she asked, "What?"

"Told 'im that I loved him."

She gave me a high five. "I know that's real. He's the bomb. You better stop fakin' on him."

I smiled. "I know. And guess what else?"

She put her hand on her hip. "What?"

I pulled my keys from my purse and jingled them. "He bought me a car."

She yelled. "Stop playin'!"

She hugged my neck and practically yanked me around in a circle. "Girl, he ain't no joke."

Suddenly, her excitement subsided. She gazed into space. "Damn, some girls have all the luck."

I smirked. "I wouldn't say that."

I looked at my man sitting at a small table alone. I grabbed her hand. "C'mon, you sittin' with us?"

She smiled. "Nah, go ahead. I'm going to stay up here at the bar."

As if I was abandoning my girl, I took short steps away from her. I turned to see her downing another drink. A miserable relationship can drive a woman to destruction. I shook my head, because I wondered when that time would come around for me again.

I sat beside John as he chatted on his cell phone. I rubbed his back. He spoke kindly. "Yeah, I'll come get him."

When he hung up, he turned to me. "Baby." He paused. "Keisha is going out and she . . ."

I smirked. He sighed. "She wants me to get JJ. I can either catch a cab, and let her take me home or we can roll out of here right after you're done."

It seemed that during all of our special moments, Keisha wanted to burden us with parental responsibilities. I huffed. "Just go 'head."

He was torn between the first ladies in his life. I pouted. "I had something special to read."

He dialed Keisha. "Key, we'll be there around ten. Is that too late?"

She obviously had a lot to say. He looked afraid. Finally, he spoke. "Ten on the dot." Pretending to be irritated, he huffed. "Yeah, I'll meet you at the house."

When he hung up, I looked at my watch and rolled my eyes. "So we gotta leave in thirty minutes?"

He nodded. I stormed from the table. I found Sundi to let him know I needed to go first. As I walked back to the table, I noticed Danielle. Her misery reminded me of how much of a good man I had. I went back to the table with a different attitude. I hugged him from behind. "I'm going first. We'll be out of here in time." I kissed his cheek. "Okay?"

He smiled and rubbed my arm. "Thank you, baby."

I plopped in my chair. "Anytime."

When we pulled up to the house, I looked at the clock. We were fifteen minutes or so late. Keisha was sitting in the car. John walked over to the car. I waved and stood in the driveway. She sarcastically said, "Your mother told me you bought Laila a car. So is that it?"

John nodded and laughed. I couldn't decipher her response, probably because she mumbled something rude. Then, as if it were okay for me to hear now, she rambled off a to-do list. "He needs to take a bath. He may want something to snack on."

John hovered over the driver's side door and nodded to all her demands. I felt stupid standing there, so I walked around to the other side of her car and opened the door for JJ. I stuck my head in. "Hey, Keisha."

She smirked. "Hey, Laila girl. What's up?"

I smiled at my biggest rival. "Nothing, girl." I grabbed JJ's hand. "C'mon man."

He lazily stumbled out of the car. I grabbed his bag and we walked toward the house. I left Keisha and John outside chatting. When we got in, I fixed him a PB&J sandwich, one of the many things I'd gotten him addicted to. I set the sandwich on the table. I walked to the window and peeped out of the blinds.

What was the urgency, if she planned to chat with John for an hour?

JJ whined. "I want some milk, Lay-Lay."

I slouched into the kitchen. "Okay, baby."

I poured milk and put it on the table for him. I went back to my surveillance. Jealousy plagued my thoughts. JJ giggled. "Uh-oh."

Milk was all over the floor. I dampened a few paper towels. When I bent down to wipe up the mess, JJ's long eyelashes batted at me. "Sorry, Lay-Lay."

He knew just how to smooth me over. I couldn't be mad. I hugged him. He wrapped his short arms around my neck and jumped on me, as I attempted to stand. I stumbled backward. We laughed.

He said, "All done."

With a big toddler propped on my hip, I straightened the kitchen. I took one last peep outside and headed upstairs. When I started running the bathwater, John finally came tramping up the steps. He came in the bathroom. He patted my bottom. "Hey, babe."

I didn't respond. I called to JJ, "C'mon man."

His little footsteps came pitter-pattering. John picked him up. I folded a towel by the tub then reached for him. "C'mon."

John tried to kiss me. I turned my head and slowly dipped JJ into the tub. He splashed water. I wiped my face. John sat on the toilet and caressed my shoulder. I yanked away.

As if he had no clue, he asked. "What's wrong?"

I looked at him. "We'll talk."

"Why can't you tell me now?"

I smacked my lips and looked at JJ. John caught my signal and left the bathroom. I knelt beside the tub washing my boyfriend's son, wishing he belonged to me, dreaming that Keisha never existed. I daydreamed while JJ played in the water. Finally, I grabbed a towel and lifted him out of the tub. I held him tightly as I dried him off. We snuggled together.

I helped him put on his pajamas and lay beside him in his bed. As he prepared to say his prayer, he patted my face. "Wake up, Lay-Lay."

I laughed. He bowed his head and said his prayer. Then he began his favorite part, which always lasted ten minutes. "God bless, um . . ., Daddy, Lay-Lay." He giggled. "Granny, Pop-Pop." He proceeded to all his cousins. "Tisha, Crystal, Pharod." Finally, I said, "Amen."

I walked to the door. He yelled, "And Mommy."

I smiled. "And Mommy."

As much as I wished I could replace her, I strive to be half the mother that she is. When I walked into the bedroom, I questioned my argument.

John sat up on the bed. "What's wrong?"

I admitted, "It's just that you and Keisha's relationship makes me feel insecure."

He opened his arms. "I'm sorry. I don't know what else to tell you. I wouldn't have our relationship any other way."

My pouting seemed worthless. I put my arms around his neck. I squeezed him tightly and prayed that I could one day accept that nothing more existed between the two of them.

CHAPTER 22

Every Saturday morning John woke up with the same question. "You tryna get some studio time today?"

Though Saturday was his most lucrative day, he was willing to sacrifice it for me. Usually, I declined, because I knew I was interfering with paying slots. For some reason, this Saturday I woke up with the need to have my voice heard. I said, "Yep."

He appeared shocked. "Really?"

I nodded. He asked. "For real?"

I smiled. "Yes."

"Stop playin'!"

I smirked. "Do you just ask me that every week for the hell of it or what?"

He laughed. "Nah, I just thought you would never do it."

I shrugged my shoulders. "I'm ready."

He hopped up. "We gotta hurry up, then. I got back to back appointments after twelve."

He jumped in the shower. I quickly followed. We ate cereal, walked the dog and headed to the studio within an hour. I went over the poems in my head I wanted to read. I practiced my cadence, perfected my flow. I repeated. I changed lines. Then, I laughed to myself. Was it really that serious?

I pulled into the parking spot beside John. He looked over at me and smiled. We hopped out simultaneously. He shook his head. "I can't believe I finally got you in here."

I rolled my eyes. "Well, I'm here."

As he opened the door, he began to tell me which poems he wanted me to read. "Remember that time when . . ."

I frowned. I felt as if he was stealing my creative authority. What if I didn't plan to read that? What if this project was going to cause confusion in our relationship? I attempted to explain. "John, I hope you don't mind me reading things that are special to my heart."

"Oh nah! It's just some of your stuff, I already got music that I think would fit."

I nodded. He kissed my cheek. "Don't worry. We're just having fun today. It ain't that serious. You don't hit the studio one day and have a CD the next."

I pushed him. "I know that."

He went into the sound room with me. He helped me get adjusted. When he walked out, he sat at the computer and fumbled with his equipment. Then, he returned to the sound room. He put headphones on me. "When I count down to one, just start speaking."

I nodded. The headphones felt like a heavy snake draped over my head. He walked out and closed the door. The dark room made me feel as if no one could see me. I watched him through the glass. Finally, he counted down using his fingers. I paused. Then, I spoke.

I thought I should hear music. I heard nothing but myself. My face frowned. John nodded. He fiddled with his synthesizer. I continued. I pulled the headphones off when I finished. I walked out.

"Shouldn't I be hearing something?"

"Nah, I just want to get some clips of your voice. Then I'm gonna mix the beats in."

I shrugged my shoulders. He laughed. "Read two more and we'll work with these three for now."

I went back into the sound room. When I was done, it seemed so simple. Why had I waited so long?

He played my voice back for me. I sounded juvenile. "I don't like the way I sound."

He laughed. "I'll polish it."

He kissed me and walked me to the door. I kissed him again and asked, "See you later?"

"It'll probably be a late night. We're working on getting these packages to the distributors."

I nodded. "Okay. Maybe I'll hang out with Dani."

"I'll call you if I get done early."

Danielle couldn't get away from her man. So, I shopped until I was exhausted. I went to my apartment. With my cell phone in the palm of my hand, I stretched across the bed. Finally at one in the morning, I got the phone call I had awaited all evening.

"You sleep?"

Trying to appear bright and bushy, I cleared my thought. "No, I was just laying here."

"I'm on my way."

I jumped up and hopped in the shower. When he knocked, I went to the door wearing a thong and a wife-beater. He stumbled through the doorway. He put his arm around my waist. "Hey, baby."

We kissed. We waddled to my bed. On top of me, he kissed my neck. He talked. I ignored him. He rolled over and tried to calm my aggression. He laughed. "Hold up, baby. I want you to hear something."

I climbed on him. "Not right now."

He nodded. "C'mon, listen."

He wrestled me off him. He stood up and pulled a CD from his back pocket. He popped it into the stereo. My voice filtered through the budget speakers. I smiled. The track sounded so polished, so professional. My heart filled. I looked at him. My eyes watered. I was proud of me. I was proud of him. He stood in the middle of the floor, obviously feeling our chemistry. My rhymes synchronized with his rhythm. His beats illuminated my words. He nodded. I smiled. I wanted the world to feel our union.

As we serenaded us, he took his clothes off then climbed on me. "Do you like it?"

I kissed him. "I love it."

He said. "I love you."

I replied. "I love you, too."

He filled my cup. We made love to our love. I trembled, I overflowed, leaving a pool for us to stay afloat.

CHAPTER 23

Each time I bathed JJ, kissed him, or said prayers with him, I felt closer to him. The need to accept his mother into my world intensified. Each time he landed a soft kiss on my cheek, I understood how important his happiness was to everyone involved. Time forced me to embrace Keisha.

I woke up to JJ's arm across my face. His leg propped over mine. I peeled him off me and stretched. He tossed around. I rubbed his belly and looked at the time. I called for John. He didn't answer. Hearing a three-year-old snore like a mine worker in the middle of the day made me chuckle. I tickled him.

"Wake up, old man."

He flipped around and then mumbled. I went downstairs. John was gone. I called him.

"Where are you?"

"I'm at the stu."

"I thought we were going to brunch."

"Yeah, but I had to come down here to straighten something out. Why don't you and JJ stop by around five and we'll go to dinner?"

I huffed, but didn't argue. "See you later."

He ignored my melancholy tone. "A'ight baby."

He hung up before I sighed again. JJ and I got up and ate grilled cheese sandwiches. So much for our brunch.

Later that evening, I strapped JJ into his car seat. We drove to the studio humming to his kids' CD that Keisha demanded we listen to. When I walked in, I felt like we'd stepped into a zoo. People were flipping around, screaming. I picked JJ up to prevent any accidents. When I finally discovered John under all the hysteria, he put his arms around JJ and me. He lay his head on my shoulder. He whispered, "We did it, baby."

"What?"

"We sold 100,000 units in just four states."

Based on the excitement around me, it was clear that this was a major accomplishment. I kissed his cheek. Hoping he'd grab JJ, I leaned JJ forward to hug his father.

"That's good. What happens now?"

"Baby, that means we 'bout to blow. Distributors been callin' me all day."

"For real! I'm so happy for you."

"We are celebrating."

JJ slid down from my hip. "Are we taking the baby?"

"Hell, yeah! Let me call Keisha."

My heart dropped. I smiled. Sometimes it felt as if I was consenting to bigamy.

He held his cell phone. "Keish. What's up, baby?"

She obviously had something to tell him, because seconds passed before he said, "You ain't gon' believe it. We finally did it."

As he spat out the good news, I heard her yelling through the phone. She seemed as excited as the circus clowns flying around me. Somehow I felt useless, because I didn't fully understand the accomplishment.

I slouched down on the couch as he explained all the details to her. Why wasn't I privy to what he thought?

*　*　*

By the time we rounded up the posse and got to the restaurant, Keisha and three of her friends were there. I was the only other female in the party. Under usual circumstances, Keisha was overly friendly. I walked up to her with JJ propped on my hip. "Girl, we've been hanging out all day. He's probably tired," I said.

She offered me a fake smile. Didn't bother to introduce me to her girlfriends. Instead, she grabbed JJ and spoke to him as if I was unfit. "Ms. Laila didn't let my baby sleep today?"

He nodded his head and pouted his lips. I could have popped him in his rock. I turned around. JJ cried for me as I walked away. He bounced on her hip, "Lay-Lay!"

Keisha glared at me. I ignored the baby for the sake of her feelings. Her girlfriends whispered amongst themselves. I held John's hand and scooted close to him.

When we all finally sat down, we were seated at two large round tables in a quaint room. I prayed they would sit at the other table. Wouldn't you bet? I pulled out my chair and Keisha pulled out a chair beside me. John sat on my other side.

By the time John stood up to make a toast, we had all drank too much. He talked about the struggle, the sacrifice. He even talked about Keisha being there when it was merely a dream. Ugh!

Finally he took my hand. "After Keisha and I broke up, I focused on the music. I didn't even think I wanted a relationship. But, this woman here." He chuckled. "She's been my everything over the last six months." He grabbed my hand. "My friend. My lover. My drive." He looked at me. "I don't think you even know how much you've changed my life. It's crazy, man." He held back the emotion. "Thank you for not talking and just listening. Thank you for your creativity. Thank you for your quiet dedication." He smiled as he approached the ultimate. "And most of all, thank you for loving my son." Keisha grunted. He raised his glass again. "Here's to my First Lady."

His words shocked everyone at the table. All the guys barked, but the women didn't say a word. It was as if I'd received a Grammy that I wasn't even nominated for. I choked on my wine. Keisha's friends looked as if she deserved the award. I should have been rejoicing. Instead, I wanted to hide under the table.

Up until that moment, I had questioned him. I awaited his evil twin. I awaited his other woman. I awaited the abuse. None of which arrived. As I sat shoulder to shoulder with his ex, I wanted to trust him. I just didn't trust her. Though she'd gone to great lengths to prove to me that they were merely just friends, the envy in her eyes told a different story. JJ reached over to play with my napkin and she snatched his hand back. Why did I feel like the mistress?

The way she huffed and puffed, it was obvious she wanted to blow the union down. Could I blame her? I tried to put myself in her shoes. The reality of her feelings was much too painful to accept. I questioned the validity of my relationship. Keisha's friends' eyes scorned me, as if they were asking, "How could you?"

John rubbed my knee. "You straight, baby?"

I nodded.

"Are you cold?"

"No. I'm cool."

He kissed my cheek and whispered in my ear. "We having a private party tonight."

I felt the need to go to my place, but how could I leave him at the peak of his success? I rubbed his forearm. As he so freely gave himself to me, I hid so much of me from him. The time for the truth had arrived.

When we got home, I fumbled around in the kitchen, putting away food, packing lunch, getting water. Finally, he called downstairs. "Damn, Laila, whatchu doing?"

"I'm coming."

When I got to the top of the stairs, candles guided my steps. Our celebration promptly began.

CHAPTER 24

By the time I left work, dusk was slowly creeping up. I headed down Spruce Street. My heavy backpack practically bent me over. I hummed to the tunes playing on my portable CD player.

I could see a shadow rapidly approaching me. Afraid to turn around, I began a slow jog. Suddenly, I felt the barrel of a gun in my back. An oh-so-familiar calloused hand covered my mouth. I stopped moving. My freedom about to be erased, my eyes filled. My heart thumped rapidly. How did he find me?

People passed on the street. I signaled danger with my eyes. He leaned down and pulled my headphones off with his mouth. "Laila, my baby girl."

His warm breath on my neck sent a frightening chill throughout my body. He kissed my ear. "How long did you think you could hide?"

Could anyone see the fear vividly written on my face? Tears rolled onto his hand. "Why you crying? You not happy to see me?"

I nodded. He pushed the gun farther into my back. "Why you lying?"

I shook my head. "You are lying!" He clamped his teeth together. "I should kill you right now."

He chuckled. "I'm not going to kill you. I'm just gonna take you home. Okay?"

I nodded. "Now, we're going to make a U-turn and go back to my car."

I nodded. "Don't be stupid, 'cause I'll kill you. I swear."

We slowly turned. The winter air blew on my moist face. I wish John could save me. I was anxious to escape, willing to die before I complied. As if I were cutting into steak, I gnawed his hand. He yelled, "Ouch!"

I bolted away. I ran for life. I ran for John. My backpack was like heavy sandbags, sinking my effort. I yelled, "He's trying to kill me! Help!"

People stood like zombies, just staring at me. Suddenly, I looked around to find that my feet were moving rapidly, but I hadn't gained any yardage. I screamed, "He's going to kill me!"

The question mark on the faces of the passersby told me that my words were not audible. Then, as if he stole my voice, I could not hear myself. Engulfed in trying to get away, I began wildly swinging my arms. Tears flung from my face. "Help me! He's going to kill me! Help me!"

Suddenly, bound by a pair of warm arms, I felt safe. John rocked me. "Shh . . . Laila. It's okay." He ran his hands through my hair. "You're having a nightmare."

Guilt consumed me. How could I expect to trust anyone when I was the liar? I planned to tell John everything about my life when I woke up.

The sun felt like a police flashlight shining in my eyes, demanding the truth. I swung my forearm over my face. When my eyes adjusted to the light, I looked at John sleeping so peacefully. So many lies, so many stories. How could I repair the damage?

I pulled the covers over my head. Why did I blame myself for a life I had no control over? I searched for the words. Finally, I shook him.

"John."

He stretched and rolled over. His back faced me.

I rubbed his shoulder. "Baby, I have something to tell you."

He grumbled. I didn't know how to begin. I didn't know if I even wanted to begin. I stared at the ceiling fan spinning round and round. Why is there such a thing as karma?

I propped my chin on his shoulder and put my arm around his stomach. I sighed. I thought. I awaited the words. I rolled out of bed and grabbed my best friend, my only friend: my notebook. I started writing. What could I say? What did I want to say? I started a poem. I rewrote it. I renamed it. Nothing seemed right. If I couldn't write it, there's no way I could say it.

I went into the bathroom and ran some bathwater. The water flowed freely. Why was I still enslaved? I sat in the tub and sank down until the water came up to my neck. Maybe I could just miraculously drown. I studied the pattern on the tile. Why is life such a maze?

John stumbled into the bathroom. He stood over the toilet, exposed. I crossed my arms over my chest. "Hey, baby."

"What's up, baby?"

"Why you up so early?"

I shrugged my shoulders.

"I thought you were gonna beat me up last night."

I played stupid. "Whatchu talking about?"

He washed his hands and started shadow boxing. "Help me! Help me!" He laughed. "Shit. You was fucking me up and had the nerve to be screaming help. I should have been calling for help."

I smiled.

"What were you dreaming?"

"I don't even know. I think someone was after me."

"Well I don't have to worry about you going out without a fight."

When I got out of the tub, I wrapped a towel around me. I climbed in the bed with John. He stared at the television. I rested in his arm, staring at the ceiling. He rubbed my damp hair. In attempts to divert the guilt, I asked, "John, do you think Keisha still wants to be with you?"

"Sometimes."

His response scared me. If I told him that my entire history was a lie, he could easily run back into her arms. If I waited any longer, he would resent me.

"Do you think you could ever be with her?"

He simply stroked my hair. No answer. I repeated. "Do you?"

"I used to."

"When did you stop?"

He laughed. "What's up with all the Keisha questions?"

I flipped over onto my stomach so I could look into his eyes. "It just looks like both of you wish you'd stayed together and I just don't really understand why y'all broke up and . . ."

"You don't have to worry about us getting back together."

"Really?"

He stared at the television. "A man can do all the dirt he wants to do, but when a woman does it in return." He shook his head. "We can't forgive 'em, ever. We understand, but we could never be with 'em again. I mean we could be with 'em, but never on the scale it was before."

He sat up as he delved further into his explanation. "I really don't care what a woman has done in her past, but the minute I enter her, she's my virgin and I don't want nobody else in my territory."

As if the thought of Keisha cheating still plagued him, the inflection of his voice rose. "How can you say that your body is your temple and shit, and be fucking three different men at one time?"

He looked at me as if he expected an answer. I raised my eyebrows. "I'm not trying to hear that shit."

"Did you cheat on her?"

"Yeah."

"She forgave you, right?"

"Obviously not, she got revenge."

I sighed. Why did the situation still seem to anger him?

"So, after you found out she was cheating, did you just let it go?"

"No. I tried. But every time we were together, that shit was on my mind. I tried to forgive her. I wanted to forgive her, but I couldn't."

"Wow. It just seems like y'all have so much love for each other. It's just scary."

He kissed my forehead. "I have mad love for Keisha. We were together since we were sixteen and didn't break up until I was twenty-five. That's like half my life."

He laughed. "Shit. We're more like brother and sister than anything."

"How did you find out she was cheating?"

"People know me and people talk. So, I followed my leads and caught her red-handed."

I didn't care to discuss the specifics. How was I to explain my case?

"Is there anything you want to know about me?"

He shook his head. "Not unless it's something that happened in the last six months. Otherwise, I don't really care."

"You don't want to know anything about my past?"

"Nope."

"Why?"

"I know you got what I want today. That's all that matters."

"What if I was married before?"

"Were you?"

I giggled. "No."

"It wouldn't even matter."

I rested my head on the pillow and hid behind my elbow. "I have some things that I want to tell you."

He appeared uninterested.

"I know I told you that I have very little family. Right?"

He nodded. "Well, I really don't have any family at all," I said.

He laughed. "Don't tell me you killed your whole family."

I smiled. "Stop playin'. I'm tryna be serious. I grew up as a foster child." I paused. "I started strippin' at fifteen." I awaited his reaction. He didn't flinch. I continued. "Then at eighteen, I moved in with a man who promised to take care of me."

I paused. How could I describe David? He wasn't the monster that he appeared to be. "He tried to love me the best way he could, but he didn't know how. He didn't trust me out of his sight, so whenever he felt the need to get me in line, he would . . ." I sighed. "He was just crazy. We would fight for no reason at all." My eyes blurred. "I came here to get away from him."

John smiled. "Laila, didn't I tell you that I study people before I approach them?"

I nodded. He tickled my chin and smiled. "Your poetry tells your whole life story."

"Why didn't you ever say anything before?"

"None of that shit is your fault. I just wanted to show you love and let you know life doesn't have to be that way."

I rose to my elbows. "So you knew I was lying?"

He pinched my cheeks. "I knew you weren't comfortable talking about your past, at least explicitly. It's all in your writing though."

I half questioned, "Is that right?"

He nodded. "Yep."

"So, you don't see me any different?"

He chuckled. "No."

I kissed him. He pulled me on top of him. My towel fell off.

"I'm your family now."

"I love you."

He massaged my breasts. He paused. Then, he laughed.

I stopped moving my hips. "What?"

"You need to dress up that grandmother story. It got too many gaps."

I curled my lips. "Leave me alone."

"Maybe you won't have to tell that story anymore."

I closed my eyes and absorbed my life. "Maybe."

He grabbed my thighs and bounced me on him. "It starts here."

His utensil peeped from its hiding place. I moaned. "Okay."

I nodded and rode my prince in shining armor off into the sunset.

CHAPTER 25

I seemed to be shopping my life away and eating even more since John had been on the road promoting his music. I invited Danielle and the kids out to dinner. When she came into the restaurant, Shandi was propped on her hip.

"Where's Jacob?"

"With his daddy. Can you believe it?"

"I guess you guys are doing okay."

"As long as I sit in the house with him, he's fine. The second I go visit my mother or come see you, he goes crazy. He's crazy."

"But you love him."

"He's all right."

We laughed. The waiter brought over the corn muffins. I helped Shandi gobble down the basket of muffins, as I gathered my thoughts.

Danielle asked, "So what's up with my boy?"

"Girl. He's on a promotional tour. I only see him like two or three days a week."

She frowned. "Um. That's not good."

I laughed. "Whatchu mean?"

"You better secure your ground, girl."

Men are going to do what they want to do. How do you secure your ground? I shook my head. "You're a trip."

"You need to handle your business."

"And do what?"

As if it were the obvious solution, she rolled her eyes. "Have his baby."

People take childbirth for granted. I sighed. "It ain't that easy."

"Whatever. Men are stupid. That's the easiest way to trap him."

I ended her rampage with one statement. "What if I can't have kids?"

She looked stunned. "Can't you?"

I shrugged my shoulders. Afraid to expose my weakness, I huffed.

"Laila, have you ever tried?"

I nodded. With one eyebrow reaching for the sky, she asked, "And what happened?"

I sighed. "I had four miscarriages."

She had a disturbed expression on her face. I smiled. "It used to bother me, but I've come to accept it now."

As the words left my mouth, I knew I was lying.

She gave makeshift advice. "You probably just have to be on bed rest."

"Tried that. Didn't work."

She wanted to help me find an answer, but there was none. "Does he want more kids?"

I nodded.

"Have you told him about the miscarriages?"

I shook my head.

"Why?"

"I guess I'm scared."

"You don't think he'll understand?"

"He'll understand, but will he want to stay with me, knowing I can't have kids?"

"You never know. I would just take it easy."

"I'm on the pill. I'm scared to try again."

"I'm sorry. That dude is worth trying again."

"You think so?"

"Hell yeah, cause when he blows up, girls are going to be on him. If you have his baby, he always gotta deal with you."

Her point was well made. I decided to take her advice to heart. Before I lay down that night, I looked at my pills. I opened the pack. I closed it. When my phone rang, I took it as a sign that I should leave the pack closed.

"Hey, baby."

I blushed. "Hi."

"I miss you."

If I owned a part of him, would it reduce the loneliness I felt? I pressed the phone to my ear wanting to feel him. I sighed. "I miss you too."

CHAPTER 26

My monthly visitor was two weeks late. I hadn't taken a test. It seemed like a curse. Whenever I took a test, I'd lose the baby within a day or two. I sat at work on my birthday and wondered how long it would be before I'd feel those unwanted cramps in my stomach.

Ann called me, "Laila, John's on the phone."

"Hey, baby."

"Hey. I got a problem."

"What?"

"I'm not going to make it home today. And I wanted to take you out for your birthday."

"John, you know I don't trip about my birthday."

"I'm sorry. I told my mother to feed Rocky. So don't worry about going over there after work."

My heart sank. I longed to be in his arms. I whined. "Okay."

"Happy birthday."

I curled my lips. "Thanks."

"I'll see you tomorrow."

Danielle called me almost seconds after I hung up with John. "Whatchu doing for your birthday?"

"Same thing I did last year."

"John ain't taking you out?"

"He's out of town."

She hissed. "He's always out of town."

"I know."

"Have you been trying to, you know?"

I giggled sneakily. "I think I am."

"For real! Have you been taking it easy?"

"Yes."

"We'll talk tonight. Let's do something chill."

"Okay."

"I'm going to come get you."

"That's cool."

Danielle picked me up around nine. When I got in the car, John called. "Baby, I'm so sorry. My mother didn't make it to my house. Can you stop by and walk Rocky?"

"Sure, baby."

He apologized again. I tapped Danielle's arm and rolled my eyes. She looked suspicious.

"I'm going over there right now."

She frowned. I mumbled my good-byes. "Can you take me to John's? Nobody walked my baby today."

She huffed, apparently irritated by the detour. I offered her gas money, but she didn't accept.

I turned the key in the door. Danielle stood behind me. I pushed the door open. Confetti flew. Balloons everywhere. A huge crowd of people yelled, "Surprise!"

John snapped a picture of me. I stood there in disbelief. I was paralyzed. John's friends were all there. My acquaintances from the poetry club were there. Keisha and JJ were there. I'd never had a birthday party in my life. When I finally snapped out of the shock, I ran over to John and kissed him.

"Thank you, baby. I love you. I love you so much."

As always, he downplayed his efforts. "Ain't nothing, baby."

JJ came over and blew his party horn. "Happy birthday, Lay-Lay."

I bent down to kiss him. "Thank you, li'l man."

"I want some cake."

I grabbed his hand. "Show Lay-Lay where the cake is."

The lady with wings, the same picture that John had drawn on my card when we first met, was on the cake. *Happy Birthday Angel* was neatly written on the cake. "Aw . . ."

I thanked everyone. Most of all, I thanked Dr. Freid for giving me the opportunity to come to Philly. A DJ was set up in the living room. Fried chicken, buffalo wings, seafood salad, deviled eggs, meatballs, and all kinds of desserts filled the island. A guy was rolling cigars in the family room. It was an upscale event, all for me. Every time John passed me, I kissed him. After twenty-four years, I had my first birthday with my first family.

Sundi came up to me. "Laila, I just wanted to stop by and give you my blessings. I have to run, but I wanted to tell you that you have really blossomed. I'm very proud of you."

"Thank you."

As he exited, Jordan entered. My jaw dropped to the floor. "Happy birthday, girl."

He hugged me. I was speechless. Finally, I said, "I'm so happy you came."

He kissed my cheek. "I wouldn't miss it for the world."

"How did you find out?"

He pointed to John. "He really loves you, Laila. See, I knew you'd find a good man."

I pushed him. "Let's not talk about that."

I directed him to the food and drinks. "Eat up."

Jordan fell right into the mix. Danielle, on the other hand, appeared to be struggling. Keisha's friends showed up and mingled amongst their glamorous selves. Danielle sat in the corner. I plopped down beside my girl. "What's up? You okay?"

She nodded. "Why aren't you mingling?" I said.

She shrugged her shoulders. I looked around the room. "Girl, do you see all these guys in here?"

"Yeah."

"They would love to talk to you."

"I don't think I'm their type."

"Why?"

She nodded her head in the direction of Keisha and posse. "They like superficial chicks like that."

"Girl, whatever. I'm not superficial."

She snickered. "You got that commercial look about you too."

I flicked her dreads. "Whatever. With these bright red tips, I think you're commercial too."

We laughed, but she stayed in her corner. I dragged one of the artists from the studio over to chat with her.

As I sashayed around the room, John summoned everyone to sing "Happy Birthday." My eyes circled the room as people congregated in the kitchen. People smiled. They sang to me. They celebrated my life. I looked at John. Tears filled my eyes. Keisha handed me a knife and I grabbed John's hand. He wiped my tears and kissed my forehead. "Cut the cake."

My arm trembled as I proceeded to cut the cake. John wrapped his arm around me and guided me. As we handed out cake, John pulled a small gift bag from the pantry. He handed it to me.

"Is it okay to open it now?" I pulled the tissue from the bag. I felt multiple CDs. I pulled one out. The shrink-wrapped CD had my silhouette on the cover. The title, "Words From an Angel," was written across the picture. As I absorbed the gift of love, the gift of sacrifice, others began to surround me.

"Ooh!"

"Let me see!"

"Oh my God!"

I hugged John and we escaped to our own world as the party continued around us.

"Thank you so much, baby."

He kissed my cheek and let me go. "Anything for you, baby."

Finally, I was convinced.

The DJ mixed Mary J and Method Man's "You're All I Need." Keisha pulled John to the middle of the floor. "Jay, this used to be our shit."

They danced. I pretended not to notice. When the song was over, I felt John behind me. He kissed my neck. "C'mon, baby. Dance with me."

While we grinded on the dance, Keisha started gathering her things. She came over and broke up our intimate moment. "See y'all. I have to take li'l man home. It's bedtime."

I was happy to see her go. John obviously felt differently. "Lay him down upstairs."

"No, I'ma take him home."

We hugged JJ and they left. With our chaperone gone, John and I were free to dance the night away. From periodic glances, I saw that Danielle was having a better time. The house slowly emptied. John helped the DJ carry his equipment out. When they finished, he handed the DJ some cash and walked him to the door. I followed.

When the door closed, I pinned him to the door. I reached up his T-shirt and kissed his chest. "You are so good to me."

"'Cause you're good to me."

I dropped to my knees and blessed my man with my gratitude.

CHAPTER 27

John dropped me off in just enough time for me to get ready and get to work. It was hard for me to believe that someone could love me that much. I gloated all day at work. The time away from him was killing me. I rushed to the studio when I got off work. When I pulled up, I was surprised to see Danielle's car parked outside. I opened the door. The guy that I hooked Danielle up with was sitting on the couch alone in the front.

"Hey, where's Danielle?"

"Back there."

I walked into the back. John fiddled with the synthesizer and nodded his head intensely. Danielle watched in admiration. I was taken aback. I looked at him. My eyes questioned her. "Hey."

"Hey, Laila."

I was uncomfortable with her knowing my secret and being alone with my man. Insecurities tapped on my shoulder. I walked over and kissed him. I looked at Danielle. "What are you doing here?"

"Greg asked me to come down here."

John removed his headphones. "How did you set your girl up with Greg?"

I shrugged my shoulders. It wasn't as if I planned to make a love connection. "I didn't even know his name. It wasn't like that."

"You know that dude doesn't have any money."

"You know I don't get into all of that."

I turned to Danielle. "Do you like him?"

She laughed. "He's all right, but I can't mess with a dude without a car."

"So did he tell you he didn't have a car?"

"No."

John chimed in. "I told her."

Why was he so concerned about Danielle's love life? I huffed. "Well, it's not like Danielle really plans on taking him seriously." I glared at her. "Right?"

"I might."

She stood up. "Lemme go out here with him."

She walked out. I sat on John's lap. "How long was she in here with you?"

"Not long."

"What's not long?"

"She came in here to say hi and we started talking. She told me she was here to see Greg." He laughed. "I was trippin', because, of everybody, he's the last dude I would hook up with anybody. He's broke and ain't trying to help himself."

"So she figured she would just sit in here with you?"

He smiled. "I know you're not jealous."

I pouted and batted my eyes.

"Laila, you don't have nothin' to worry about."

I rolled my eyes. He kissed me. "Okay."

I nodded.

He asked, "Did you eat?"

"Earlier. You want me to cook or you wanna go out?"

He rubbed my lower back. "Let's go out."

He stood up and headed to the door. I slouched behind him and he put his arm around me. I cuddled close to his chest. As we passed Danielle, her eyes shot darts at me. A suspicious chill ran through my veins.

"See you later."

She waved. I questioned her commitment to me. I swallowed deeply to dispose of the thought.

When we went out, I reminded John of all the food left over from the party. "Let's just go to your house."

He walked toward the truck. I headed to my car. "Laila."

I looked over my shoulder. "Are you gaining weight?"

I laughed. "No."

"You look phat to death."

I opened the car door. "Whatever."

He squinted his eyes and whispered, "You sexy as shit."

I pulled off and he followed.

When we got to the house, I pulled food from the refrigerator while he chatted on his cell phone.

I warmed the food and set his plate in front of him. Finally, he gave me his undivided attention.

He smiled. "That was my realtor."

I nodded.

"When the house is finished, are you moving with me?"

I asked, "I don't know. Do you want me to?"

"You know what I want. I want you to stay here, but you wanna be so 'independent.'" He used his fingers as quotation marks to emphasize the word.

We laughed. "I'm sorry. I don't mean to be like that."

"You need to learn how to trust me."

He held his hand out. I held it and walked closer to him. "I do trust you."

He put me in a playful headlock. "No, you don't."

Maybe my trust issue had very little to do with him and more to do with people in general.

Awakened by cramps, I lay on my side facing the bedroom door. Why was God doing this to me again? Another failed attempt. When the pain became too much to bear, I rolled off the bed and stumbled into the bathroom. I sat on the toilet. My panties were clean.

Afraid to strain, I sat patiently. After I finished, it seemed the cramps had disappeared. Could it be that it was just a false alarm?

When I slipped back in the bed, I wondered if I should tell John. Suddenly, the alarm clock hollered in my ear. John jumped. He reached over me and turned it off.

"What time does your plane leave?" I said.

He mumbled. "At seven."

He fumbled around the room. I wanted to help, but I couldn't move. He jumped in the shower. I sat up in the bed and I rocked back and forth. Finally, I got up and checked his bag to make sure he had everything. I hovered over his luggage. He came in, wearing his towel. "My baby's always looking out for her man."

I smiled. "Always."

The driver came to pick him up around five-fifteen. I stood at the door and watched him load his luggage. I rubbed my tummy and prayed that the baby inside me would stay for his return. He waved. I blew a kiss.

CHAPTER 28

At thirteen weeks my stomach was still flat. The baby grew in my hips. John's constant travel kept him out of the loop as to if and when I had a period. I sat in the doctor's office, excited that I'd finally made it over the first trimester.

I sat on the table, waiting for the doctor to come in. I flipped through *Motherhood* magazine. Finally, I thought my time had come. The doctor walked in, he covered my belly with gel, and ran the probe over the area. He smiled. "There it is."

I looked at the screen. I couldn't make out the body parts, but there was life. The heartbeat thumped loudly. Waves of motion were visible. He pointed to the screen. "Can you see it?"

Tears filled my eyes. I nodded.

"Everything looks good. Do you want to know the baby's sex?" he asked.

I quickly turned away from the screen. "Nope. I want to be surprised."

He wiped my stomach and asked me to come to his office when I was dressed. I expressed my concerns about the possibility of still losing the baby. He offered positive advice and suggested some books. He sealed it with, "I don't think you'll have any problems. There could be many reasons why you miscarried before, but for me to know exactly why, I would have had to run a test on the embryonic sac fluid. Since I wasn't your doctor at the time, we just have to keep our fingers crossed." He scribbled on his prescription pad. "Keep taking the progesterone and I think you'll be fine." He handed me the prescription. I could have done cartwheels out of the office. Instead, I skipped to my car.

Just as I was about to head to work, I decided to go back to John's house. I called him to see if he wanted breakfast.

When I got there, he came downstairs wearing his boxers. "Why aren't you at work?"

I handed him his food and winked. "Because . . ."

He kissed me. "Because what?"

"I don't know how to tell you, but . . ."

He poured some orange juice. "Just say it."

"I'm pregnant."

He choked. "For real?" I nodded. "When did you find out?" he asked.

I sat down. "Well, I've known for a while, but . . ."

"What's awhile?"

I answered. "Like two and a half months."

With a puzzled look, he asked, "Why you wait so long to tell me?"

"I was . . ."

He frowned and shook his head. "I know you wasn't thinking about an abortion."

"No . . . I was afraid that . . ."

He interrupted me again. "I would be mad."

I laughed. "Lemme finish."

His excitement flattered me. "You right. Go 'head."

"Some years ago, I had a miscarriage and I was afraid that it could happen again."

"C'mere, baby." He reached out for me.

I stood in front of him. He hugged me as I explained. "I think I'm out of the danger zone now."

"So, how many months are you then?"

"Three."

He chuckled. "Keisha's gonna trip."

During every major milestone in his life, she was the first person he considered. I didn't comment.

He held my shoulders and looked at me. "My baby mama."

We laughed. "I guess you have to move with me now," he said.

I shrugged my shoulders.

"My baby can't stay in that little room with you."

"Let's get the baby here safely first."

"We're gonna get him here safely all right. We gonna keep you off your feet."

I shook my head. He always went over the top. As if the question finally popped in his head, he stopped. "Did you think I couldn't handle it if you had a miscarriage?"

"I thought . . ." I paused. "I think that you would look at me differently."

"Laila, you should know by now that I don't trip off certain shit. As long as you don't step out of line, I'll never look at you different."

All I ever wanted David to admit was that it wasn't my fault. Yet, he blamed me. Somehow he made me feel like my sexcapades before we met were the reason I couldn't hold a baby. John's compassion made up for all the days that I had felt less than a woman.

CHAPTER 29

My belly began to stick out at around twenty-five weeks. When I began to receive suspicious stares, I felt obligated to make it known. One morning, I stepped into the office, prepared to make my announcement. My desire to confess was obviously written all over my face. Ann smiled at me.

"Morning Ms. Laila. How's that fine boyfriend of yours?"

I blushed. "He's good. Just really busy."

She laughed. "That's the price of success. Huh?"

I nodded. "Well . . ."

She giggled. "I guess you'll be a stay-home mom with his schedule."

I raised my eyebrow. "What?"

She propped her face up on her hand. "Laila, I have three kids. I know what pregnancy looks like."

I laughed. It's funny how some people can rub you like sandpaper, then after working with them for a year and a half, you find yourself loving them. I rolled my eyes. "Ann, how long have you known?"

She laughed. "Well, at first I noticed your evil PMS mood swings had stopped. I thought that was because you were in love. Then, I noticed your hips. When you started working here, you were a toothpick." She curled her lips. "Now you look older than seventeen. You're filling out."

She lifted my top. "Let me see. I've been dying to see if your belly started poking out. These shirts are deceptive."

I laughed and let my stomach muscles relax. It felt like I'd just unbuckled a pair of tight jeans. She rubbed my belly and covered her mouth. "Laila, your stomach is big. I can't believe you were hiding it so well."

When Dr. Ryder walked in, he asked, "What's going on around here?"

We laughed. Ann mouthed. "Are you going to tell him?"

I nodded. Instead, she took the privilege of spilling the beans. "Dr. Ryder, we're going to have a baby."

He frowned. "Who's we?"

I raised my hand. "That would be me."

He nodded. "Really. That's nice to hear."

He proceeded to walk back to his office. A part of me felt embarrassed. Why did I feel bad when this was everything I wanted? I followed him into his office. "Dr. Ryder, I . . ."

He smiled. "I'm happy for you, Laila. Was it planned?"

He threw me off guard. "Um . . . um . . . sorta."

He nodded. "Oh, so are you getting married?"

I shrugged my shoulders. He planted a seed of uncertainty in me. He nodded again. "Wow, so you planned a baby. But no wedding."

I felt stupid, but I knew John loved me. We just never really talked about marriage. Maybe it was more important to have an extension of him, than to be an extension of him. I nibbled on my bottom lip as I stood there with nothing to say. I frowned. Why was I seeking his approval?

"Well, you young people do things differently."

I chuckled. "Yeah, I guess you're right."

He swooped his hand over his hair. "I wish you the best. If you need anything, let me know. Okay?"

I nodded. "I will."

I turned to walk out and he called me back. I swung around

hoping he had something positive to say about my situation. "Have you told Dr. Freid yet?" he asked.

I smiled. "No, I plan to call him today."

Hoping Dr. Freid would be more compassionate, I slipped into Jordan's office to call him. I excitedly sang. "Hi, Dr. Freid."

"Laila. This is strange. I was going to call you today."

"Really?"

He cleared his throat. "Yes. A young lady came by here yesterday, asking about you."

My heart dropped. "What did she want?"

"She believes you're her sister."

Just as I embarked on a brand new life and buried the past, I hear this. "What?"

"She looked a lot like you. She claims she's your sister."

Baffled as to why she would go there, I stuttered, "What did she say?"

"She wants to meet you. She asked if I could get in contact with you."

My stomach bubbled as I asked, "Did you give her any information?"

He chuckled. "No, I told her that I'd see if I could find you and to come back next week."

Who was this girl? How did she find me? I needed to know everything about her visit. "What else did she say?"

"Not a lot."

"How did she find me?"

"I really don't know."

Could this be a scam? Was David involved? After almost two years, could he really still care? Uncertain of the legitimacy of this girl, I said, "Don't tell her anything."

He added. "She said your mother wants to meet you."

My heart floated in my stomach. "What's my sister's name?"

"Paula."

I wanted to know more, but was afraid to know anything. "Did she leave her information with you?"

"Yes, it's . . ."

"Hold up. Let me get a pen."

I wrote the info on a small piece of paper. How could a mother wait twenty-four years before thinking about her child?

"So, how are things otherwise?"

His news distracted me. I couldn't remember why I called. I sighed, "Things were really good, before I got this news."

"Laila, I thought this would be good news."

"I don't know. I'm wondering if David is involved."

As if that thought hadn't crossed his mind, he paused. "For some reason I don't think so. She looked a lot like you. The resemblance was striking. I don't know. I think the girl is definitely related to you."

Coming from a white man, could I really believe it? Did she really look like me or was she just another black girl? I stared at the number and kept scribbling "Paula" on the paper. I asked, "What was so striking?"

"She was about your color. Nice-sized girl. She had long dark hair, just like you. In fact when she walked in, Jodi asked if she was related to you. And that's when she told us why she was here."

I sighed, "Wow."

My fear was smothered by curiosity. I had to see this girl. I wanted to know more about her. So what if it was David? John would protect me. I gave Dr. Freid a brief overview of my life, excluding the pregnancy, and rushed off the phone.

I kept thinking about the family I spent my whole life dreaming about. Just when I finally accepted that they didn't exist, they appeared. As if I had forgotten that I was at work, I called John. "Baby."

"What's up?"

"I called Dr. Freid and . . . I . . . ."

"Yeah, and . . ."

"Some girl came looking for me yesterday."

"And . . ."

"She claims to be my sister."

John laughed. I snapped, "Why are you laughing?"

"Do you believe him?"

Agitated by his nonchalant attitude, I huffed. "It's not about whether I believe him. Do I believe her?"

"What did she say?"

I gave him the details. He sighed. "Whatchu wanna do?"

"I don't know."

"Are you scared?"

"I'm scared that she isn't my sister. It could be somebody that my old boyfriend is manipulating."

"Fuck him. I know you ain't worried about him."

I didn't respond. He shouted. "You worried about him?"

"Yes."

"What do you think he wants to do to you?"

I mumbled. "Kill me."

He laughed. "Ain't nobody gonna kill you. Trust and believe that."

When Dr. Ryder tapped on the office door, it was clear that I had to defer the conversation. Questions haunted me all day. If Paula was legitimate, could she answer them?

The paper with her information was tucked in my bra. Maybe my heart could determine if she was who she claimed to be.

I went to the studio after work. I pulled John into his office. Before I spoke, he asked, "So what did you decide about the girl that's supposed to be your sister?"

"I don't know . . ."

"If you weren't worried about ol' boy, would you call her?"

I hesitated. Then, I nodded.

He rubbed my hair. "Call her, then."

I grimaced. "What if . . ."

"Didn't I tell you I'll protect you?"

I nodded. Did I fear David or did I still love him? Did I really think he'd kill me? My mind was in turmoil. Did I really want this girl to be my sister? What was I really afraid of?

"Call her."

He handed me a cordless phone. I stood up and paced in circles. I pulled the number from my bra. John laughed. I dialed 1. Then, I hung up.

He stood up and wrapped his arms around me. "If you ain't ready, don't call."

"Do you think I'll ever be ready?"

He shook his head. "Probably not, but you gotta confront it. Don't you want to see her?"

"Who?"

"Your mother."

Was I really ready to come face to face with the woman who abandoned me? Without further delay, I dialed the number.

Paula answered. "Hello."

"Hi, is this Paula?"

"Yes, who's this?"

"My name is Laila. Laila Jackson."

She paused. "Laila. I'm so glad you called me."

John studied every syllable exiting my mouth. "I heard that you were asking about me," I said.

"Yes. I've been looking for you for a long time."

Silence graced the phone. Finally, she continued. "I don't know how to explain everything to you, but I know you're my sister."

Her matter of fact tone scared me. Her voice reminded me of my voice on my CD. My hands trembled. I asked, "How do you know this?"

"Were you born on March sixteenth, 1980?"

I gripped the phone tighter. "Yes."

"My mother," she sighed, "our mother knew your birthday. So I asked the nurses at Jackson Memorial about the baby that was left there on that date."

I couldn't bear standing any longer. I sat on the couch. John walked over and rubbed my shoulders.

"They wouldn't tell me anything. Then, an older nurse came to me and said she named you. That your name was Laila and she lost track after you got into the system. So I went to Social

Services to see if you were adopted or if your name changed."
She chuckled. "They ain't give up nothing. That got me nowhere. So, my mother told me to go to the library and research
newspapers from that time." She sighed. "And there it was. The
nurses named you Laila Jackson."

I shook my head. Hearing my story from outside-in made me
cringe. She continued. "The librarian showed me how to search
for you on the Internet. As soon as I put your name in, the chi-
ropractor's office popped up."

That Web site was made so long ago and was never updated.
Thank God. She continued. "When I clicked on it and saw your
picture, I prayed it was you. I used my last dollar to pay someone
to take me to Pompano Beach." I sighed. "I had to see you in
person."

As her story circulated through my veins, I felt sedated. I felt
her sincerity. This was my sister. As much as I was scared, something else in me said this was real. There was silence on the
phone as I attempted to accept what was going on. "Paula, how
old are you?"

"Twenty-two."

"Who raised you?"

"I was raised by our mother."

I corrected her. "Your mother."

"Laila, I know you have a lot of questions, but my mother has
full-blown AIDS and she's going to die any day and I was wondering if you would come visit her. It's her last wish."

I contemplated. She asked, "Are you still in the Miami area?"

"No."

"Are you close enough to get here?"

"Paula, I don't know what to say."

She pleaded. "She did a lot of things in her life, but she wants
forgiveness. Give her that chance."

I sighed. "Paula, how was your life?"

She huffed. "I didn't have a childhood. My mother was on and
off drugs all my life. She has seven children. I was the last of

seven. I was the only child she raised. I don't know why she wanted to keep me." She took a deep breath. "I wished she hadn't."

"Have you found your other brothers and sisters?"

She chuckled. "There are three girls and three boys. She don't even know half of their birthdays."

Disgusted by her lack of concern, I rubbed my stomach and shook my head. "That's crazy."

"So far, I've found you and another sister. She's four years older than you."

I sighed. At moments, she sounded like a forty-year-old woman. She continued. "She's had several close calls, but she's still fighting. I don't know how long she'll be alive. If you can get here, please come as soon as possible."

I promised Paula I'd call her back. I hung up the phone and dropped my head between my legs. John massaged my back. "What did she say?"

After feeling alone in this world for the majority of my life, I felt sick. I looked at John and all that I felt needed to be said was, "I have six brothers and sisters."

He massaged my shoulders. "What made her call you now?"

I told him about my mother's condition. He twirled his fingers in my curly ponytail. "Are you going?"

I was anxious, but hesitant. There were so many questions, but most of all I wanted to know why. Why would anyone leave a baby out here to fend for itself?

I mumbled, "I don't know."

Coming from a close family, he struggled to relate. "Do you want at least to see her?"

I used to dream of what she'd look like, how she'd smell. Finally, I get my opportunity and she has full blown AIDS, a complete distortion of my fantasy.

I rocked back and forth. "Do you think I should go?"

"I would."

I turned to face him. "Will you go with me?"

He winced. "When?"

I snapped. "You don't have to go."

"No. I want to go. It's just that I have events set up for the next month or so."

When I needed him most, he couldn't be there with me. How could I return to Miami alone?

As he stroked my back, he apologized. "I'm sorry, baby."

Trying to sound convincing, I folded my lips. "No. It's okay."

He beamed off into space. I propped my elbow on the armrest and balanced my head. "I think I want to be alone tonight."

As if it mattered at the moment, he asked, "Are you going to perform tonight?"

I shook my head. "No, I wanna be alone."

He pulled on my arm. "C'mon, baby. You've been so happy. Don't let this get you down."

Ignoring his fake compassion, I diverted attention to him. "When do you leave again?"

"Tomorrow."

I stood up. "I'll talk to you before tomorrow. Okay?"

"C'mon Laila. Lemme be here for you."

He wrapped his arms around me. I pulled away. "I need to be alone."

After a slight struggle, he realized that I wasn't giving in. Finally, he granted me my freedom and kissed my forehead. "Call me if you need me."

I nodded. He stood at my car door. "Do you want me to come over later?"

I shook my head. "No, I'll call you when I want to talk. Okay?"

I left the studio, picked up Chinese food, turned my cell phone off and locked myself in my apartment. I wrote to help mediate my anger. Finally, I drifted off to sleep.

CHAPTER 30

When I woke up, it was twelve o'clock. I jumped up, turned on the shower, and pulled out my scrubs for work. When I grabbed the phone to call in, I realized it was midnight. I sat on the bed to stop the racing speeding through my body. I poured a glass of water.

When I turned my cell phone on, the alert message said eight messages. Danielle left three messages about the poetry club. John left five. When I listened to John's desperate messages, I felt horrible for excluding him. He wanted to help. It just seemed logical to me that he'd want to cancel one of his travel dates to be with the woman he claimed to love.

I called him, but didn't get an answer. I tried the house. Still, no answer.

I brushed my teeth and packed an overnight bag. When I left the house, it was close to one in the morning. I stopped by Pathmark to get breakfast food. When I got to John's house, all the lights were out. I came in the front door and it looked like Rocky had vomited on the kitchen floor. Yuck!

I mopped the mess up. Rocky's face sagged more than usual. I wiped his mouth off with his towel and spread newspaper in his cage. After I emptied the cleaning bucket in the backyard, I washed my hands. More work than I had expected in the middle of the night. When I clapped for him to get inside, he whined.

I chuckled. "Get in here, old man."

Suddenly, I had a taste for peanut butter and jelly. I made my favorite meal and sat at the table and added a few lines to a poem I'd started earlier.

After I ate, I sluggishly made my way upstairs. The room was dark. In efforts not to wake John, I tiptoed around the room while I undressed. I went into the bathroom to brush my teeth. When I walked over to turn the stereo off, John grunted. I patted the comforter to let him know I was there. A feminine moan crept from the sheets.

I mumbled, "Baby?"

She yelled, "Oh shit!"

A head on *my* side of the bed popped up. Wild dreadlocks crowned the silhouette. The PB&J I'd just downed was in my throat. I stumbled over and flicked on the light switch.

Danielle covered her face with the comforter. My body wouldn't move. John slept peacefully. My mouth hung open. All of the air in the room evaporated. A fish out of water, I struggled to breathe. My heart crumbled into tiny pieces. The debris felt like tiny knives stabbing every organ in my body. In between gasps, I said, "Danielle?"

She didn't respond. I screamed, "John!"

He rolled over. I yelled, "Danielle!"

Slowly, she peeped out. "I'm sorry, Laila."

Her voice brought tears to my eyes. I screamed. "Get out. Get the fuck out!"

I stormed around to John's side of the bed. I shook him. "John!"

He yawned. He stretched. I smacked him with all the strength I could muster. Danielle's naked body scampered around, grabbing her belongings in one bunch. She stumbled down the stairs.

John jumped out of the bed. His penis dangled from his body.

How could he sleep with my friend? How could that bitch sleep with my man?

I pounded on his bare chest. He grabbed my forearms. "Calm down. It's not what you think it is."

I cried. "What is it? You're fucking my girl?"

He wrestled me to the bed. I curled up in the fetal position. I sobbed. "How could you do this to me?"

He hovered over me and stroked my hair. "I'm sorry. I don't even know what happened."

My tears soaked the comforter. He sat beside me. "I love you. I don't know what happened."

"How long have you been fucking her?"

He hung his head. I screamed, "Put on some clothes."

He grabbed his shorts from the floor. "Baby, tonight was the first time."

I wanted to know more. Then again, I didn't want to know anything at all.

He rubbed my back. "I was drinking too much at the club and your girl . . ."

I covered my ears. "John, don't tell me anymore."

"Lemme explain."

My chest heaved. "I can't handle it."

I stood up and stormed out of his room. He followed. "Please baby, don't . . ."

I slammed JJ's bedroom door in his face. I crawled into the twin bed and wept. When I finally learned how to trust, I was betrayed by the only family I had.

I lay there, pregnant with his baby. How could I leave now?

I cried the night away. John paced the hallway. He went back and forth to the bathroom. When I opened the door in the morning, he rushed to me.

"You all right?"

Feeling enough anger to spit in his face, I snapped. "What do you think?"

He grabbed me. He held me. Wishing I had enough strength

to fight him off, I leaned my head into his chest. He is all I have. "How could you do this to me?"

He apologized again. I put my arms around him. "John, it hurts so bad."

He kissed my head. "I'm sorry."

"Why Danielle?" I struggled to comprehend. "Why her? I always knew it would be someone, but my girl!"

As if stupidity made his knees buckle, he slouched on the steps and gave me a dumbfounded stare. "I went to the club, hoping that you would change your mind and stop by."

I frowned. He rubbed his eyes. "I know you said you wanted to be alone, but I thought you might have gone there. I kept calling you, but you . . ."

He huffed. "Anyway, I had too many tequila shots. I was a little drunk and ol' girl said she was gonna follow me to make sure I made it home safely. When we got here, she said she needed to use the bathroom." As if he regretted it, he grunted. "I let her come in. And . . ."

He shook his head. "Next thing I know, she was in my bed. Then, you came."

I searched for the truth. Afraid of what I might see, I turned my head and mumbled, "I'm going to Miami."

"For how long?"

I glared at him. "Does it matter?"

"I just wanna know."

"I don't know. I just have to get away. I think it's time for me to find my family."

He offered to buy me a plane ticket. I declined. "I wanna drive. I need time to think."

He frowned. "Baby, that's too far. I don't want you driving that far."

I turned my head. "It doesn't matter what you want me to do."

He tried to debate with my wishes as I headed to the bathroom to shower. "Laila, you're going to be driving for days."

I sucked my teeth. "So."

He stood in the doorway. "When are you leaving?"

I rolled my eyes. "As soon as I can get my shit and get out of here."

He begged. "Laila, why? Let me go with you." He tried to reason with me. "We'll get a plane ticket and go together. We'll leave today."

I looked him in the eyes. "John, I am leaving today. I don't care what you do." I chuckled. "It's funny how yesterday your schedule was too busy, now you can go."

As I started closing the door, I gestured for him to leave. He huffed and backed out of the way. My face looked like a punching bag. I washed my face and got in the shower.

When I walked out of the bathroom, he handed me a printout. "Here are the directions. It takes eighteen hours to get there." He flipped through the pages. "I bought you a plane ticket. You don't have to use it if you don't want. I just want you to have a choice."

As if he thought his generosity would get him out of the dog house, he smiled. I tossed the papers back at him. "No, thanks. I'll get my own directions."

I walked in the room and packed some of my things. He staggered behind me. After I packed the essentials, I walked into his office and sat at the computer. The airplane confirmation was still on the screen. I printed it out just in case. Then I went to MapQuest.com to confirm it was actually eighteen hours. He was right. Damn if I had it in me to drive that far, but I planned to make him believe I would. I stuffed the flight confirmation and the sheets of paper with the directions in my purse.

He stood in the doorway like a lost puppy with his arms folded. I brushed past him, grabbed my bag, and finally said, "I'm leaving."

I trotted down the stairs. He followed. "Are you sure you don't want me to go?"

I posed and looked him up and down. "Aren't you going out of town?"

"I already missed my plane."

As I poured orange juice, I snickered. "So you can just miss your appointment like that."

"Right now, I don't give a fuck about a damn appointment. We gotta get this right."

I chuckled. "When I asked you to go with me yesterday, it was impossible. Now that you fucked my girl, all that matters is me."

He just stared at me. I rolled my eyes. "Where are the keys to the truck?"

He grabbed the keys from the key rack. "Don't leave me, Laila."

"I'm going to Miami. I'll call you when I get there."

"You promise?"

I nodded. He walked over to kiss me. I turned my head. I pulled my keys from my purse and tossed them at him. They fell on the floor. He bent down to pick them up. "You need money?"

I nodded. He rushed upstairs and returned with five hundred dollars. "You have my other bank card, right?"

I nodded. He handed me the money. "Use whatever you need."

I nodded. He brushed my hair behind my ear. "I love you."

I walked to the door. Before I rationalized, I said, "Love you, too."

He stood in the door wearing his boxers, like his dog was lost and he didn't know where to look. I looked over my shoulder and waved, a sign to assure him that I wasn't gone forever. I threw my bag in the truck and pulled off.

I stopped in the office and begged Dr. Ryder to understand. He didn't object. In fact, he told me to stay in Miami as long as I needed. My flight was at six-fifteen in the evening. With hours to drive in circles, I used the opportunity to think about my life and what I deserved and if I even deserved to be here.

CHAPTER 31

As I drove around town, John called again and again. I didn't answer. Another Philadelphia number popped up on my phone. I answered.

"Hey Laila, it's Keisha."

I rolled my eyes. "Hey, Keisha."

"John told me what happened and . . ."

Afraid that she was gloating over my pain, I sighed. "I really don't feel like talking about it."

"Laila, I know how you feel, but I called you to say keep your head up."

I curled my lips. "Thanks."

"I know he loves you." She paused. "He's just a hot ass."

As if that was what I needed to hear, I huffed.

"He doesn't mean it."

I chuckled. "Keisha, did he tell you he was with my friend?"

"He told me everything and he doesn't have a reason to lie to me." She sighed. "Sounds like your girl is a ho. She's who you need to be mad at."

Hoping his ex could be a pathway into his psyche, I asked, "Why would he do something so stupid?"

"Laila, I don't know. He tells me everything and I don't think he's ever cheated on you before. And to be honest, he's far from stupid. He's not the dude that would intentionally sleep with your friend. Trust me. I know. He keeps his shit away from home. He's the type of man that if you don't look for it, you won't find it."

I grunted. She continued. "I'm not saying that he's doing anything. In fact, I know he hasn't done anything." She sighed. "And I have to admit, there was a time when I was jealous of you. I wondered what you had over me. Why did he cheat on me and not you? Then, I realized we were young. People grow up. Jay has really grown up. I think last night was a mistake." She paused. "I hope you give him another chance."

I was baffled. Was she sympathetic or envious? Did it make her feel better knowing that he finally cheated on me? "Keisha, why do you care?"

"I love John. I love him with all my heart and I see how much he's changed with you. I don't know if you know, but I cheated on John." She awaited a reaction. Then, continued. "He was bitter for a long time. Then, he met you and somehow you made him trust women again. His happiness directly affects my baby's happiness."

Chills ran through me. I wasn't certain if she was sincere, but it felt real. I wished one day to be so considerate. "Keisha, you're amazing. How can you love a man like that and see him with another woman?"

She chuckled. "Girl, he will never forgive me for what I did. He's blatantly told me that he could never be with me. So, as much as I used to hope we'd get back together, I know we won't. Why shouldn't somebody else be happy?" She took a deep breath. "I used to try and make his life miserable, but it didn't get me anywhere. So, I just chilled and now our friendship is much more than I could have ever dreamed of."

Her strength never ceased to amaze me. I sighed, "Wow."

"Don't sleep, Laila. I think you have a lot to do with why I'm so relaxed."

"Really?"

"You're a good person. Anyone who takes care of that bad son of mine the way you do is cool with me. Shit, if you leave John, we could both end up with some ignorant ass chick around our kids." She laughed. "Seriously though, Jay loves you and if I were you, I'd give him another chance." As if she regretted the mistake she made, she paused. "Laila, don't do anything stupid. They can dish it, but they can't take it."

Why was the world so unfair? I nodded. "Keisha, thanks. I'll talk to you when I get back to Philly."

"Any time, girl. Make sure you take care of that baby. See ya."

Finally, I parked the truck at the airport and caught my flight. When I arrived in Miami, it was around ten o'clock due to a long delay on the runway. I got a rental car and got on Interstate 95. With no destination, I just drove. When I saw exit 7, I got nervous. Eighty-first Street was my old stomping grounds. Initially, I planned to head farther north to get a hotel a little outside of Fort Lauderdale. Instead, I hopped off at the exit 7. I had no purpose, I just needed to see it.

I circled around the North Miami neighborhood. I passed the old hole in the wall where I used to dance. I shook my head. Boy, had I come a long way. As much as I hated to admit it, David saved my life.

I drove back on Interstate 95 North and found a hotel in Fort Lauderdale. When I got settled, I pulled the bedspread back and lay on my back. Complete silence. Finally, I heard my thoughts. I picked up the phone and called John.

The phone half-rang before he answered. "Hey, baby."

"Hey."

"Are you okay?"

"Yes, I decided to catch the plane."

As if he was relieved, he sighed. But I felt like he already knew. "That's good. I wish you would have let me come."

Trying to minimize the conflict, I said, "Shh. I needed space. I needed time to think."

"How do you feel?"

"It hurts."

He winced. "I wish I could make it better."

I smacked my lips. "You can't."

"I'm sorry."

After more than a year of being my best friend, I didn't know what to say to him. I wanted to suppress the pain. The thought of Danielle lying in my man's bed on *my* side invaded my mind.

"Have you called the girl?" He corrected himself, "The girl, Paula."

"No, I'll call her tomorrow when I wake up. I'm tired. I'm really tired."

"I know. I wish I was there."

I huffed. We wouldn't even be in this situation had he agreed to come when I first asked. I rolled my eyes and said my goodbye. He begged me to stay on the phone. "John, I'll call you tomorrow."

He sighed. "All right, baby."

It was just about ten-thirty the next morning when I woke up. I showered and drove to the IHOP. With my short stack of pancakes smiling at me, I suddenly lost my appetite. With all the hysteria, I'd completely forgotten that this could be a prank. How could I be so quick to trust at a time like this? I shook my head at my own naivety. I didn't bother to bring anything to protect myself with. After a few deep breaths, I called Paula.

"Hello . . ."

"Hi, Paula."

"Laila."

"Yes. How'd you know it was me?"

"I just hoped it was you."

"Paula, I need you to promise me that this is not some kind of game you're playing with me."

Her voice weakened. "What do you mean?"

"Did anyone pay you to find me?"

"Laila, if you were born at Jackson Memorial and someone left you there, I know you're my sister. We can go as far as a blood test for all I care. I've heard about you all my life."

"Do you know a guy named David Dubois?"

"No, should I?"

Why question my instinct now? "Never mind. I'm in Miami."

"Oh my God! Where? I'll meet you somewhere."

"No. I'll come to you."

"I'm at the hospital. Can you just come here?"

"What hospital?"

She snickered. "Jackson Memorial."

It was strange how we were reuniting in the place where my mother abandoned me. I confirmed. "I'll be there in thirty minutes."

"Okay, I'll wait for you outside."

I pulled up to the Visitors' entrance. She stood there patiently. She had folded her arms as she looked left and right. The resemblance shocked even me. Her slim legs looked like two twigs in her denim miniskirt. Her short T-shirt exposed her belly ring. She wore a long ponytail. If I didn't know, I would've assumed she was my twin.

The baby flipped inside of me. My chest burned. When I finally stepped out of the truck, I felt faint. As I approached, she smiled; beautiful white teeth nestled in flawless brown skin. My heart told me she was my sister. Eye to eye, we stood. I stared. She stared.

She threw her arms around me. "Laila, I'm so happy you came."

I admitted, "I'm really scared. I don't know if I'm ready."

"It'll be okay. Trust me. You deserve this."

I nodded. She rubbed my paunch. "Are you pregnant?"

I nodded. "Then you definitely deserve this. Let's go."

We walked into the hospital. I stopped her. "What's her name?"

"Adele Sylvince."

My heart sank deeper each time the elevator stopped. Finally, Paula stepped off. I followed. She held my hand. Until I saw the name on the room door, a distorted part of me wished David would appear.

I grabbed her arm. "Paula, does she know I'm coming?"

"She knows."

I took a deep breath. She asked, "You ready?"

I walked into the room. Paula said, "Ma, she's here."

I heard her breathing before I saw her feet. Finally, I stood at the foot of her bed. Tears rolled from her eyes. She reached her hand out to me. She looked to weigh about ninety pounds. I cringed. She whispered, "Please."

I stared at her. Her skin looked like black leather. Thin strands of hair decorated the top of her head. Her eyes were sunken. My eyes watered. She struggled, "Please."

Paula took my hand and walked me around to her. Adele covered her mouth with her mask and coughed. I stood at her side. She touched the top of my hand. I drew away. She closed her eyes. "I'm sorry."

I looked at her as if she'd already died. I studied her features. She cried. Paula rubbed my back.

"Isn't she beautiful, Ma?"

She nodded. "Just like I remember."

Stunned, I asked. "You remember how I looked?"

She nodded. "You was my sixth baby."

Tears streamed down my cheeks. I recognized a Haitian accent as she continued, "You were so precious, but I was scared. I wanted to keep you."

She choked. Paula helped her spit into the tube. "I thought someone else deserved you more than me."

Spit bubbles lined her lips. "I'm sorry. I wanted to find you a long time ago."

Paula agreed. "She did. She always talked about you. She don't remember none of her kids like she remember you. She called you Angel."

I covered my mouth. It was the same name that John had given me. My mother nodded and then smiled. "Angel. You were so precious."

Finally, I asked, "How could you leave all your kids?"

She wiped her tears. Paula answered. "She was on drugs. She was a prostitute. She didn't know any better."

She nodded in agreement. Paula seemed overly protective of her. I envied their relationship. Adele clutched my hand. "Please forgive me?"

I shook my head. "I cried every night until I was ten. I used to dream you'd come find me. I lived in over a dozen homes in my life. Other children at least knew their mother's name, knew something about them." I tried to restrain my anger. "They had pictures of their mothers. I didn't have anything." My lips trembled. "How could you do that to me? If it wasn't for a man I met at seventeen, I would probably be laid up here beside you."

Just as I said it, I knew I owed my life to David. Despite his frequent abuse, he saved me from death on the streets. He deserved more credit than I'd given him. I darted from the room. I heard her choking on her spit. Paula helped her and ran into the hall to find me bawling in front of the nurses' station.

She hugged me. "Laila, I know sorry doesn't make up for anything, but she really is."

"When did she realize she was sorry? When she was about to die?"

She nodded. "I know how you feel."

The range of emotion I felt was unexpected. When I looked into my mother's eyes, I saw reflections of my childhood. Hate stirred in my heart and I wanted to yank out her breathing tube. Her apologies enraged me more.

I gasped for air. "I'm sorry, Paula. I didn't mean to excite her."

She rubbed my back. "She knew it was gonna be like this. Her other daughter doesn't even want to see her. At least you came."

She wiped my tears. "Do you think you want to go back?"

I nodded. We walked back in the room. As Paula and I got acquainted, Adele watched us. She seemed to find joy in our friendship. As we compared childhood stories, I accepted that Adele may have done me a favor.

Her eyes shifted from one to the other of us. She seemed

peaceful. We left around five. Paula asked me to stay at their place. I agreed. She rode with me to get my things and directed me back to their little rundown project in Miami. Was it too late to stay in the hotel? I had never lived in such horrible conditions. And I had lived in some rough areas. The peach stucco projects looked as if they were abandoned.

When Paula opened the door to their little pad, I shivered. The clutter in the tiny little space gave me the creeps. She apologized. "Sorry for the mess." She pushed stuff out of the way. "I've been at the hospital so much."

"You really love her, don't you?"

She nodded and smiled. "She was always the child." She chuckled. "I can remember being like four-years-old," said, and then she scratched her hair, "and her being in pain cause she couldn't get her dope. I would put a cold rag on her head. Give her aspirin. Whatever I had to do to make her better. I've taken care of her my whole life." She sighed. "Nothing's changed."

I shook my head. "Damn. That's crazy." I thought aloud, "I wonder why she wanted to keep you, knowing she couldn't take care of you."

"She was clean when she had me." She smiled. "When she ain't on drugs, she's a good person."

I smirked.

"She would always tell me we were going to find Angel when she was clean, but before we would try to find you, she was getting high again."

I mumbled. "Was it all bad?"

She smirked. "It was hard."

I reflected on my life, as did she. The awkward moment ended when she asked if I wanted to see some old pictures. We rummaged through an old shoebox. Most of the pictures were taken at parties. On most shots, Adele wore two long braids that hung below her small breasts. Both Paula's and my body type were identical to Adele's. When I asked Paula why there were no pictures of her as a kid, she joked, "How can a junkie take time to take pictures?"

We laughed. She pointed out, "Wasn't she pretty?"

I nodded. "What happened? How did she start getting high?"

"It's a long story. Her family came here from Haiti when she was eleven. Her father used to prostitute them."

"Whatchu mean?"

"You know. He would make her and her sister prostitute for money for the family. And they were scared of him. So, they did it."

"Damn."

"Um-huh. She had her first baby at fifteen. And they made her give that baby to the man that got her pregnant."

"Did she ever see the baby?"

She shrugged her shoulders. "She don't know where he is now. She ran away after that."

"Damn."

"Yeah, she got a whole bunch of stories to tell," she said. "She been through a lot."

She smiled. I sympathized. "It's a good thing she had you."

"Yeah, I don't know if it was good or not." She chuckled. "I went through a lot."

"It sounds like it."

She nodded. "I've been through everything. I even sold my body for her. I've copped drugs for her. Everything." She hung her head. "I've fought for her." She lifted up her shirt. "You see that."

There was a long scar down the side of her stomach. "I got stabbed fooling with her."

I cringed. She added, "It's been rough."

"How long has she been sick?"

"She's been sick for a long time. She tested positive like six years ago, but she stopped taking her medicine over the last year."

"Why did she stop?"

"She said she was tired." She shrugged her shoulders.

"Do you work?"

Paula nodded. "Yeah, I work at the grocery store."

"Did you finish high school?"

She shamefully hung her head. "Nope."

"Don't feel bad. You're a survivor."

She blushed. "Thanks."

We shuffled through the pictures. A photo sizzled my fingers. I dropped it. Déjà vu. Oh my God! My insides burned. I rubbed my eyes. I stood up and took a breath. I paced the room. I picked the picture up again. The same juvenile pose. The same teenage girl. The same tight pink sweater. The same smile. Anxiety rippled through me.

Paula asked if I was okay. I shook my head. "Paula, if she was fifteen when her first child was born, how old would that child be now?"

"I think her first son would be . . ." She counted on her fingers. "He would be thirty-one."

"Paula, are you sure?"

"Do you know his name?"

"I don't think she knew his name."

I covered my mouth. "Remember the guy, David, I talked about in the hospital? He has the same picture."

She looked suspiciously. "Are you sure?"

I rolled my eyes in my head. "Positive."

David kissed that picture every morning. I knew the lady on that picture. It must have been prior to her being forced to sell her body. This picture looked different from all the other ones. I redirected the question to her. "Are you sure this is her?"

She nodded. "Positive."

As I worked this all out in my head, Paula looked confused. "What was he doing with the picture?"

Afraid to believe that I could have been having sex with my brother, I shook my head. "His father gave it to him. He said she was his mother."

Her eyes bugged out. "Laila, no! What are the chances?"

I looked at her and repeated. "What are the chances?"

She ranted. "This shit is too crazy. So if that's the case, then you . . ."

I nodded as she came to the revelation that I was struggling to deal with. My insides did somersaults. I wanted to vomit. Ugh! Visions of us making love haunted me. Was he really my brother or was this a big mistake? My head pounded. No! This was a crazy nightmare.

Paula covered her mouth as she sat and watched me agonize over my incestuous relationship. Finally, I admitted. "I was fucking my brother."

When I put the obvious into words, Paula grunted. "See, that's why we need to find our brothers and sisters."

She shuddered. "How long were you with him?"

"Too long . . ."

"Are you going to tell him?"

I shrugged my shoulders. "Whatchu think?"

"Why not?"

I told her about my experience with David. Initially, we both agreed to let it go. As the evening progressed, I decided it would be best if I called him. Doesn't everyone deserve to know the truth about their existence?

I stood outside of the place I once called home. Blood pumped vigorously to my heart. I put my finger on the doorbell. I prayed. Finally, I pressed.

His footsteps rushed to the door. I started to run, but I got the courage to stand. He opened the door. His mouth dropped open. His eyes welcomed me home. He looked down at my belly. Disappointment covered his face. I reached for the knob on the screen door. He pushed it open. I stepped into the house. He grabbed my hand.

"I'm sorry, Laila."

His words sounded sincere. He hugged me. "I'm so sorry."

I nodded. "David, I . . ."

"I'm happy you're okay."

"I am, but I . . ."

"I loved you."

"I know, but . . ."

"I never meant to hurt you."

"It's okay, I . . ."

"I thought you would never come back. I used to dream that you needed my help. I wanted to help you, but I couldn't."

I nodded. He hugged me again. He reached his hands up my shirt. I tried to push him away. He begged. "Just hold me."

I submitted to his desperation. His fingers traveled to the elastic of my pants. I stepped backward. He held tighter. The struggle too much for me to handle, I submitted. He slobbered on my neck.

"I missed you. How could you leave me like that?"

My body responded to him. I wanted to explain to him that we were siblings, but his touch captivated me. He pulled my pants down. I didn't fight it. He raised my shirt. He kissed my stomach.

"This should be my baby."

I nodded. My brother entered me. He pounded on me, oblivious to my discomfort. When he was done, he stood up. I looked down at the puddle beneath me. A pool of blood surrounded me. I touched my stomach. Blood gushed from me. I cried, "No! My baby! No!"

I sat up. I looked around. Paula ran from her room. "Laila, are you okay?"

I gasped for air as I attempted to recall where I was. She put her arm around my shoulder. "What happened?"

Feeling ashamed, I brushed it off. "I have really bad nightmares."

"Really?"

I nodded. "I've had them all my life."

Paula got up at the crack of dawn. I heard her shuffling around the apartment. I peeped at her. She caught me. "Good morning."

I mumbled, "Morning."

"I go to the hospital around nine every day."

I yawned.

"Are you going with me?"

"I guess."

Was there really anywhere else for me to go? The dream had me petrified. It was a good idea for me to attempt to get as much information from Adele that I could. At least I wouldn't approach David with only a picture.

Paula handed me a raggedy washcloth and towel. I stepped into the cluttered bathroom. Mold covered the tiles. I delicately crept around, careful not to touch the floor with my bare feet. I dressed to the best of my ability. I opted to go makeup-free. My draping shirt camouflaged my protruding belly.

When we walked in Adele's room, her eyes filled as they did the day before. She wiped her tears. She moved her oxygen mask. "Good morning."

Paula leaned over and kissed her. "Hey, Ma."

Adele rubbed her forearm. Paula stroked her face. Adele reached out for my hand. "Angel."

"Good morning."

She smiled. My peaceful tone was intended to forgive her for all she'd done. She stared at me. I was motionless. How could I talk about her firstborn child? How could I wait? The tremble in her voice told me that I didn't have much longer.

I sat down in the chair. I rubbed her hand. I scooted closer to the bed. "Adele, I have some questions to ask you."

She nodded. She lifted her mask. "Ask me anything."

"Your first son." She nodded. "When was he born?"

"February 4, 1973."

Even if I wanted to guess the picture was a coincidence, the birthday was confirmation.

"What happened?" I asked. "Do you know where he is?"

Her breathing turned into panting. "They took'm."

"Who?"

"My father. He took my baby and he sold'm."

Not willing to believe my ears, I shook my head. David's father was such a peaceful, kind man. He wouldn't harm a fly. "Are you sure?"

She nodded. Tears rolled from my eyes. "I had that baby right in my house." She wiped her tears. "I heard him cry and they left the room. I never seen my baby after that."

"Why do you think they sold him?"

She sniffed. "That motherfucker sold everything."

I pulled the picture from my purse. "How old were you in this picture?"

She smiled. "I was pregnant with my baby."

"Do you know who would have this picture of you?"

She shook her head.

"Adele, I know a guy with the same picture. He thinks his mother died."

She stared at the television. "Adele, do you remember any of your father's friends? Do you remember their names?"

She shook her head. "I ain't seen him since they took my baby."

"Do you want to meet your first son?"

She shrugged her shoulders. Paula interjected, "I don't think she can handle that."

She blocked us out and drifted off into a daydream. Paula said that was how she'd do when she didn't want to hear the conversation. If she didn't want to meet him, why disregard her wishes?

I tried to explain to Paula, but she made her point. "It's not about her no more. We need to know so we ain't sleeping with our brothers."

I nodded. "You're right."

"So are you going to call him?"

"I don't know."

I left the room and drifted through the hospital corridors. There was so much I wanted to say, but watching her struggle to get words out was too much for me to handle.

When I returned to the room, I noticed Paula pacing in circles outside the door. My heart stopped. I needed more time with

Adele. I wanted to tell her that I'd forgiven her. I wanted to ask about my father.

I jogged toward her. The door was closed. Paula was biting her nails. "She flatlined."

"Oh my God! What are they doing in there?"

She said, "They're going to let her die."

"Why?"

She held my shoulder. "Laila, she has AIDS. They ain't gonna keep trying to save her."

Paula seemed to be at peace. "Did she talk after I left?"

"She told me that she loved me and that she wanted us to . . ." Her emotions finally broke through. She sniffed. "She hopes that we stay together."

I hugged her. "We will. Don't worry. We'll stay together."

"She wasn't the best, but she was all I had."

I wiped her face. "You got me now."

We sat down. After fifteen minutes or so, one of the doctors came out of the room. He looked at Paula. He nodded. He knelt in front of us. He rubbed Paula's shoulder. "It's over. Her time of death was ten fifty-two."

Paula nodded. He put his hand over hers. "You've been terrific."

"Thank you."

"I can only hope my kids will be as dedicated as you."

She smiled. "Thank you."

Paula sobbed. I rubbed her shoulder. The doctor told us what we needed to do next. Paula reminded him that her mother would be cremated.

Feeling a slight connection to this woman, I asked, "Do you want to at least have a memorial service?"

"We ain't got money for all that."

"Do you want to have a service?"

She shrugged her shoulders.

"She had a rough life. Let's give her a peaceful departure," I said.

"Where we gonna get the money?"

I stroked her hair. "I'll get the money."

We called a few funeral homes to get the price of a simple service. After we got the best price, I called John to tell him. He asked if I wanted him to bring the money.

He whined. "Why don't you want me with you?"

I huffed. "John, it's too much for me to deal with right now. Lemme bury my mother and then we'll talk."

He sighed. "Where are you?"

"I'm in Miami."

"Where?"

I sighed. "That's not important."

"All right, there's enough money on that bank card to handle that. So, just charge it. Okay?"

"Thank you."

"Laila."

"Yes."

"I love you."

"I love you too, baby."

When I hung up, Paula seemed impressed. "Damn, you got a man like that."

I shook my head. I questioned my relationship. I shrugged my shoulders. "I thought he was a good man, but I don't know anymore."

"Is he always there for you like that?"

"Yeah, I guess, but . . ."

"He's a good man, then."

The vision of him and Danielle rendezvousing haunted me. I looked at Paula. "He slept with this chick that I thought was my best friend a couple of days ago."

"What?"

I nodded. She shook her head. "Girls ain't shit."

"What about him?"

"Men gon' be men, but you ain't supposed to fuck your girl's man."

I'd already conceded that Danielle was history. As wisdom came out of my younger sister's mouth, I wondered. Will men always hurt you in some form or fashion? Is it their self-centered nature?

If I looked at the overall package, John was as close to perfection as anyone could get. I wanted to forgive him, but how could I teach him a lesson?

We sat in the Waffle House and chatted more about life, John, and everything else in between. There was something special about staring into eyes that resembled mine. I loved her. I felt she belonged to me and I belonged to her. I was so thankful that she found me. The envy I felt about her being the chosen one vanished. Her life was no better than mine. From that moment on, I promised that both our lives would shift into a different direction.

We went back to the apartment. Paula called Adele's friends to let them know. We planned a small intimate funeral. Her obituary was quite simple. She lived. She struggled. She died.

I wrote a poem of repentance and added that to the program. If I repented for her, would that mean she was forgiven by all? I hoped.

Paula switched to what I didn't want to discuss. "Are you going to call David?"

"I'm scared."

"Do you want me to call him?"

"I don't know what we would say, because he thinks his mother died when she gave birth to him."

"Well, we need to tell him the truth."

"Do you think he'll still be mad at me for disappearing on him?"

"Hopefully, he won't see you like that when he finds out that you're his sister."

I shrugged my shoulders. "Hopefully . . ."

"So what are we going to do?"

I picked up the phone. "I'll call him."

My heart raced, but the moment arrived for me to confront my fears. I looked at the time. He would probably be at the office. So, I dialed the old cell phone number.

After one ring, he picked up. "David Dubois."

My stomach swirled. I took a deep breath. "Hi David. This is . . ."

He instantaneously recognized my voice. "Laila."

I sighed. "Yes, I…"

"I'm showing a house. Can I call you at this number?"

I thanked God for the break, so I could revive myself. I rushed into the bathroom and rinsed my face. Paula came behind me. "What happened?"

"He's gonna call me back."

"When?"

"He was with a client."

"Do you think he'll call back?"

We sat patiently by the phone for almost an hour. Finally, it rang. I tossed the phone to Paula. She answered then handed me the phone.

He sounded irritated, "What's up?"

"I need to talk to you."

He chuckled. "Laila, I don't have time for this. You disappear. I don't know where you are. I don't know if you're dead or alive. Now you call me damn near two years later talking about let's talk."

"It's not what you think it is."

He huffed. "What is it? You on the streets again and you need a place to stay?"

"It has nothing to do with me."

"If you were unhappy, all you had to do was tell me. You didn't have to carry it like that."

"David, I'm sorry. I shouldn't have, but I was afraid of you and you know it."

"So, why are you calling me now?"

"Because I found out something about your mother."

"Don't play games with me," he said.

"I'm not. I found my family and I . . ."

He snickered. "You found your family."

"They found me."

"Um-huh. So what's up?"

"Can you meet me somewhere?"

He agreed. I invited him to the apartment. He wouldn't be able to fully appreciate what I was telling him unless he flipped through the photos himself and felt her essence in the cluttered apartment.

David knocked on the door around seven. Paula looked at me. I looked at her. I motioned her to the door. She jumped up and answered. He walked into the dim apartment.

I stood up. I wasn't sure if I should hug him or not. I did. He didn't reciprocate. "Come in."

I sat on the couch. Paula sat beside me and David sat across from us. He checked his watch. I giggled within at his arrogance.

Then, he finally looked at us. "I guess this is your sister."

I nodded. I grabbed Paula's hand, seeking that sister-girl strength. "Yes. She's my sister."

He admitted. "Damn. Y'all look just alike."

We smiled at each other. I picked the picture up from the table. "And this is our mother."

I slowly flipped it over and handed it to him. The picture was much clearer than the wrinkled one he owned, but it was definitely the same person. He looked at the picture. He chuckled. "Don't play games with me, Laila."

I raised my eyebrows. "Where would I get that picture from?"

As reality sunk in, he shook his head. "This is crazy." He looked at the picture. He looked at us. He looked at the picture, then back at us. "She looks just like y'all!"

I nodded. As if he could not believe his eyes, he rubbed them and squinted. "How can she be your mother, if she . . ."

Before he completed his question, he realized his answer. He chuckled again. "Stop playing games."

Paula stepped into the conversation. "David, I don't know you or know anything about you. But, I do know that's my mother on that picture. If you think she's yours, then we are brother and sisters."

As if he refused to believe it, he shook his head. "I don't

know. My father could have gotten that picture from anywhere. I might have the wrong picture."

We both glared out. He rambled on why we were possibly wrong.

Then he noticed. "You pregnant?"

I nodded. "Six months."

His mouth hung open. As the truth settled in, his angry streak surfaced. "You mean to fucking tell me that my father lied to me all my life?"

I shrugged my shoulders. "I don't know. Maybe he was told that she died, too."

Smoke rose from his ears. "He never wanted to talk about it." He hit the wall. "He never said anything. All he said was she died."

We watched silently as his rage heightened. "I'ma kill him."

He wiped his forehead and directed his anger at me. "And who the fuck you pregnant by?"

I spoke calmly, "David, calm down."

He beat his fists into his hand. "Laila, why?"

I stood up and walked to him cautiously. I hugged him. He wept on my shoulder. "Laila, tell me this is a joke."

"I wish it was, David. I really wish it was."

"What should I say to him?"

I sighed. "Do you really want to say anything?"

He heaved. "What the fuck do you think?"

I backed up and pleaded. "David, please calm down. Please."

Paula looked frightened. I was petrified. I tried again. "David calm down. I'm sure your father had a reason. I'm sure."

He stumbled back into his seat. As he wanted to erase the nightmare we were all a part of, he dropped his head in his hands and wiped vigorously. "This is some weird shit."

Thankful that I was capable of calming him, I patted his back. "I know."

He spoke calmly, but angry words came out. "I just might kill his ass. I could kill his ass. I always knew he was lying. I just didn't know why." He turned to me like I was his confidante. "You know."

I nodded. "He's a good father. You can't kill him. We don't know the whole story."

We sought to calm David for almost an hour. Paula finally told him how Adele had him. He wondered if his father was his biological father or not. Paula believed that Adele's father sold him to the biological father.

"What does your birth certificate say?"

"It says his name. And my mother's name says Mary Sylvince."

We glanced at each other. "Sylvince is her name, but where did they get Mary?"

I shrugged my shoulders. It was clear that we were all brought into the world by the same woman. I felt robbed, but David felt betrayed by the man he respected. When he left, he was almost in tears. I walked him to the door. He hugged me. He groped my face. "It's no wonder I loved you so much."

I nodded. He added. "I still love you. You know that, right?"

I nodded. "When you left, I drank and drank. I didn't want to believe it. It hurt so bad," he said.

I didn't respond. He kissed my cheek. "Maybe you had to leave. Imagine if we were together when we found this out?"

I nodded.

"You never answered me. Who are you pregnant by?"

"He's a good guy."

"I wish I could have made you happy."

I nodded.

"I'll call y'all tomorrow about the funeral arrangements."

When I finally closed the door, I leaned on it. Paula asked, "Are you okay?"

I nodded. "That was hard."

"Yeah, it was. Do you think he'll kill his father?"

I shrugged my shoulders.

"Do you think he's capable of killing somebody?"

I laughed. For the first time since I'd known him, I didn't fear him. "Yes, I think he could kill somebody."

"Are you serious?"

I nodded.

"We should've gone with him."

"Girl, we've done our duty."

She looked at me. I reminded her. "I told you how he used to beat my ass. I wanted to get him out of here while he was calm."

"Maybe he was so angry because he never had a mother. Maybe he hated women."

"You got a point."

CHAPTER 32

It's so amazing how black women know how to be fly with limited funds. I watched Paula dress for the funeral. She looked like she belonged on the cover of *InStyle* magazine. She slipped into a black pencil-cut knee-length skirt. She wore a plain white T-shirt. Long wooden and metal beads looped around her neck to adorn her basic outfit. She stepped into her four-inch heels and smoothed her skirt. She glanced in the mirror and noticed me watching. She smiled.

I said, "You look good."

She lowered her head. "Thanks. So do you."

I looked down at the black smock draped on my expanding body and shrugged my shoulders. "Thanks."

Up until ten minutes before the funeral began, it appeared that Paula and I would be the only ones in attendance. Slowly, people strolled in. Paula pointed to various people.

"That was her girl. They used to trick together. She been clean for a long time, though."

Most of them fixed up nice for the funeral. Others straggled in as if they walked in off the street. We watched the door. David appeared in the entrance. Paula pinched my leg. I smiled. He didn't look in our direction. Paula all but jumped and yelled his name to get his attention. Finally, he acknowledged us. She summoned him. He refused and sat in the back.

The minister stepped up to the podium. "Let us pray."

We bowed our heads and held hands. In the middle of the prayers, I heard Paula sob. She took our clasped hands and wiped her tears. The moisture dripping between fingers warned me that I was in for a teary hour. Her chest heaved rapidly. I peeped out of the corner of my eyes. Finally, "In Jesus' name, Amen."

I helped her sit down then wiped her face with a tissue. She cried aloud. "Why, Lord? Why?"

She had been unbreakable through everything else, only to collapse at the funeral. I patted her back. She yelled, "Why?"

Partially embarrassed, I looked around the room. No one looked sad or as if they would miss her. What a miserable funeral.

Paula blew her nose. She rocked back and forth. "Why, Lord?"

When it was time for me to read my poem, I was almost afraid to leave Paula's side. I looked around for someone to replace me. No one seemed to catch the signal. I whispered, "Are you okay?"

She nodded. "Go 'head. I'm okay."

I walked to the podium. I said my disclaimer. "Most of you here who knew Adele probably are wondering where I came from." I chuckled to lighten the mood. "Well, I'm Adele's daughter and I had the opportunity to meet her just before she died." I smiled. "I thank God for that chance. Over the last couple of days, I've gotten to know more about the woman who gave birth to me. I looked at pictures of her and the thing that touched me the most was her smile. It was sincere. I only wish I'd known her longer." I hung my head. "For the first time in my life, I can honestly say that I forgive her." I paused for sympathy. "With that, I'll start my poem."

When I looked out into the small room, David frowned. I continued, "For Thee I Repent."

I creatively spoke for Adele, asking for the forgiveness of everyone she hurt, begging them to understand who she was and ultimately requesting their pity.

All the desertlike eyes that originally faced me at the beginning of the poem were flooded. I touched a soft spot in every person in the room. I looked at David. He sobbed. My heart dropped.

He wept like he was wounded. I wanted to comfort him. I wondered if he cried for me or for Adele. After the benediction, I hugged Paula. She sniffed. "I'll be okay."

People offered Paula sympathy and praised me for my poem. Yet, not a soul acknowledged that I had a loss too. David walked up to me. He hugged me. "Laila, I've been thinking . . ."

I nodded for him to continue.

"We don't know for sure that Adele was my mother and if you . . ." He hung his head. I just knew that he couldn't possibly be thinking: "If you want to try and work things out . . ."

If not for pride, I would have smacked him. I clenched my teeth, "That is perverted."

He tugged my arm. "We were together for four years and you were happy."

Trying to maintain my composure, I roared, "You were happy."

"Are you happy now?"

I put my hand on my hip. "Yes, I am."

He chuckled. "Where's your man then?"

Paula noticed the altercation. She came over to play referee. She hugged David. "I'm glad you decided to come."

He nodded. "Yeah, me too."

He glared at me. "Paula, give me your phone number. Let's stay in touch."

Something about his tone frightened me. I huffed. People shuffled around us. David's eyes pierced through me like he was the devil. It was then that I got scared. Everything around me appeared in slow motion. Suddenly, my eyes were covered from behind. I smelled his cologne. My man was there to protect me like he promised. He brushed his face up to mine. His five o'clock shadow grazed my hair. "Guess who?"

I smiled. Though I had asked him to stay away, I needed him and he came. I cautiously said, "Baby?"

He dropped his hand and turned me around. "John. How did you get here?" I said.

"You put the arrangements on a credit card. I checked the statement online." He smiled. "That simple."

I giggled. I kissed him again. In the midst of my excitement, I forgot about David. When I snapped out of my moment, David was gone. When I looked at Paula, she smirked.

"Baby, this is my sister."

He hugged her. "Nice to meet you, baby sis."

"I'm glad to meet you too, brother."

We walked out of the funeral home. I had unconsciously forgiven him for his indiscretion. I gripped his hand like an antsy toddler. When we got to the parking lot, I noticed David sitting in his car with sunglasses on. I was no longer afraid because my man was by my side, which I'm certain infuriated David.

John walked us to my economy rental car. "What's next?"

Paula responded. "We have some refreshments at the house."

"Should I follow you or what?"

"Ride with us. I'll bring you back."

We hopped in and pulled away. David followed.

When we got to the apartment, we pulled out the odds and ends that we had prepared. Knowing my upscale man, I apologized. "Baby, we wanted to keep it simple."

He smiled. "That's cool."

David walked into the apartment as if we hadn't had a confrontation at the funeral home. He sat down and chatted with some folks. I kindly introduced him to John.

"David, this is John." I stressed, "My man."

He shook his hand. "Nice to meet you."

I explained, "David is my brother."

After people had eaten and the small crowd got smaller, John massaged my neck. I looked at him. "Hey, baby. What's up?"

"What's Paula gonna do now?"

"Whatchu mean?"

"When you come back home, who she got?"

I shrugged my shoulders. "I'll make sure she's okay."

"Have you asked her to come to Philly?"

"She probably ain't tryna come to Philly."

"You never know."

He took it upon himself to ask. "Paula, you think you'd want to come to Philly?"

She smiled, but shrugged her shoulders. He whispered to me. "She could take your spot and you can move in with me."

"I never said I was moving in with you."

"You never said you were moving to the new house, but you and the baby need to at least move into the town house."

I giggled. "As long as my baby's daddy pays the mortgage, we can move in."

"C'mon now. You know how I do."

I rubbed my stomach. "We'll think about it."

"Paula, we got a nice place for you to stay," said John.

She nodded. He used his hands to demonstrate. "It's only like this big, but it's nice."

I elbowed him. "We'll take care of you. You need to have family around."

She smiled. "I really ain't got much to lose here."

He laughed. "That's what I'm talking about."

I grabbed some of the disposable serving dishes from the table. When I walked into the kitchen, Paula and John were having a private conversation. I immediately questioned his motive for wanting her to move. I looked at the both of them. I tried to shake the feeling. How could I live my life wondering if he was checking on every female I brought around?

I rinsed some of the dishes. I shook the water from my hands and turned around. In the small space that divided the kitchen from the living room, my man was now on his knees in front of me.

He reached for my damp hands. I noticed David stand up. Frustration was all over his face. My eyes wandered around the room. John gripped my left hand, "Laila. You know I love you." I nodded.

"You know I need you." I nodded.

"I feel like the happiest man in the world when I'm with you."

I looked at David. He had tears in his eyes. Mine filled. I looked at Paula. She nodded anxiously. I retracted my hand.

John whipped a small box from his suit jacket. He opened the box. Paula clapped. Others shouted a response for me. David shook his head. I was on the same page with him. I slowly shook my head. Was this just a sympathy present? Poor Laila. I broke her heart. Now, I'll ask her to marry me. His lips moved. I blocked out his voice, everyone's voice.

By the anticipation on everyone's face, I knew he'd popped the question. I looked down at him pleading for me. I stared at him. His eyes showed desperation. Could I trust him for the rest of my life?

In an effort not to embarrass the man I love, I nodded, but I wanted to shrug my shoulders. He slid the ring onto my finger. He stood up and hugged me. Our weight shifted from side to side. With his moist cheek next to mine, I tried to force myself to cry. I couldn't and I didn't.

He kissed me. Paula put her arms around both of us. "This is so sweet."

When he released me from his bear hug, I continued with my chores. I didn't stop to think about my decision. With my sister beside me, and my baby inside of me, I found what I'd searched for all my life.

CHAPTER 33

Paula lay beside me. I watched the clock. When my contractions wavered between one and two minutes, I tapped her. She yawned.

"What's up, Lay?"

"I think it's time."

She hopped up and ran around the room. I laughed at her. "Girl, calm down."

She paced back and forth. She slipped on her sweatpants. "I have to call John."

I lay there on my side, curious as to when she'd think about me. Finally, she grabbed the roller bag that I'd packed weeks ago.

"Are you wearing that?"

I nodded. Sweat beads started to form on her nose. My breath felt like it was being blocked. I slid from the bed and waddled down the stairs. Paula ran behind me. "C'mon, get in the car."

We rushed out of the garage, into the car and flew to the hospital. As we drove, she called John. She called Keisha.

When we got to the hospital, she pulled up to the emergency doors. She blew the horn. She was humorous, in spite of my pain, I opened the door. She flew around to the passenger side. She got a wheelchair. I rolled my eyes at her. "I can walk."

"Sit your butt down."

I plopped into the chair. With the car doors stretched open, she erratically wheeled me into the hospital. I sat in front of the registration desk in my plaid flannel pajamas. My legs were cocked open. Finally, they rushed me into the delivery room. The nurses hooked me up to the monitors. The doctor came in to check. I had dilated four centimeters. After the same routine every Saturday night for two weeks, I was relieved that I was finally ready. The baby's heartbeat rumbled through the machine. The doctor laughed. "He has a strong heartbeat."

Paula smiled. "So, it's a boy?"

I looked at the doctor. "I want to be surprised."

Paula pouted, "You make me sick."

John rushed in. He kissed my forehead. "Hey, baby."

He hugged Paula. "Thanks P-Diddy."

She pushed him. The pain became more than I could bear. I frowned. He asked, "You okay?"

I shook my head. I tried to reposition. A contraction rippled through my pelvis. I shouted. "Owww!"

John stood at my side. He held my hand. "Breathe, baby . . ."

I roared, "I am breathing."

He rubbed my back. I yelled. "Stop, don't touch me."

Paula laughed. I found nothing funny. I buzzed the nurse. She slowly made her way in. "Can I help you, ma'am?"

"When can I get an epidural?"

She smiled. "Your chart says that you aren't scheduled to get an epidural."

I clenched my teeth together. "I want an epidural."

"I'll have to get approval from your doctor. Then we'll get you all prepped."

Pain had filtered throughout my body. The noise in the room irritated me. "Turn the TV off."

They did. My body burned like the sun was in my room. I

peeled off my gown. "Oh my God! I'm so hot." I shouted, "Get out!"

They looked shocked. John tried to relax me. He rubbed my head. "John, don't touch me."

He nodded. Finally, Keisha came in the room. She whispered to Paula, "How's she doing?"

Paula smirked. "She tripping."

I spat out, "I'm not tripping. I'm in pain!"

Paula giggled. "Told you."

Keisha came to the other side of the bed. She ran her hand over my face. "Shh. Relax."

Her voice soothed me. "Are you getting an epidural?"

I shrugged my shoulders. "I want it."

"What's the holdup?"

John said, "Her doctor has to approve it."

Keisha walked to the door. "Whatever. Y'all just haven't raised enough hell. You'll have it in a minute."

She stormed out. Within seconds, the entire staff shuffled in behind her. The anesthesiologist told me to sit up. I followed his instructions and prayed. He inserted the needle in my spine. My eyes rolled. How did I succumb to allowing the venom to permeate my veins?

The pain mellowed. The sun rose. My family smiled anxiously around my bedside. Their voices were melodies of support. I smiled.

John pulled out the video camera. He pointed it at me. "How do you feel?"

I nodded. "I feel good."

My doctor walked in. "Good morning, family."

They spoke in unison. He looked at the screen tracking my contractions. "I think we're just about ready." He shook John's hand. "You ready?"

John patted his arm. "Yep. Make sure you get my baby here safely."

They closed the room door. They handed everyone scrubs. I

started feeling warm again. John patted my forehead with a cold compress. The doctor instructed me to breathe. The breathing lessons had escaped from memory. I got irritated. I looked at John. "I don't remember."

He calmed me. "Just breathe. Don't worry."

Paula stood on the other side, rubbing my shoulders.

"You're doing good."

Keisha was behind the doctor with the camera. I told her to turn it off, because my bowels felt like they were loosing any minute. I told the doctor. "I gotta go to the bathroom."

He instructed. "Just push . . ."

"But I . . ."

"I see the head."

John left my side to see the baby's head. The nurse said, "Push."

My entire midsection cramped. My legs felt weak. It seemed like everyone in the room yelled, "Push!"

With all of the wind in my body, I pushed. Someone announced. "The head is out."

I pushed again. Every nerve in my body relaxed. I heard a mousy cry. The sound made me shiver. The doctor said, "It's a girl!"

John clipped the umbilical cord. Suddenly I was cold and lonely as everyone shifted to the examination table with the baby. The nurse shouted, "Eight pounds, two ounces, and twenty-one inches."

I peeped over to see my baby. She looked gray under the light. Finally, John noticed me. He came over. "She's so pretty, Laila. She looks like you."

The nurse wrapped her in a receiving blanket and handed her to me. I cradled my little girl. John touched her tiny fingers. Then a brief moment of sadness came over him when he looked at my bare finger. I touched his arm, because I knew it bothered him that I had taken the ring off. As I held our baby in my arms, it bothered me too. So I assured him. "We'll be okay. I just want to make sure we're doing it for the right reasons."

He looked at the baby. "Isn't she reason enough?"

I nodded. "Let's take it slow." I kidded. "You've trapped me now. I can't go too far."

He laughed and kissed my forehead. "So, what are we going to name her?"

Before I responded, I stared at her for what felt like an eternity. I had considered various names, but decided to wait. I wanted to look at her to see what emotion she triggered in me.

As she squirmed in my arms, every possible emotion came over me. A tear rolled from my eye. My mind was immediately flooded with horrible snapshots of my own life, my own birth. A baby abandoned into the storm. A teenager who sold her body under the name Quiet Storm. An abused young woman desperately trying to escape the storm. How had I survived my entire life with no sunshine. I sniffed back the tears and took a deep breath.

I drowned the thunder from my past with the sweet coos coming from her tiny lips. It was as if she were telling me to cry no more. Just holding her gave me a peace that I never knew existed.

Finally, my search for unconditional, committed love was over. I owned her and she forever owned me. The rain was gone. I calmly looked up at the man who helped bring forth the light and said, "Sunshine."

AIN'T NO SUNSHINE

CANDICE DOW

ABOUT THIS GUIDE

The suggested questions are intended
to enhance your group's reading
of Candice Dow's AIN'T NO SUNSHINE.

DISCUSSION QUESTIONS

1. In your opinion, who actually saved Laila's life?

2. Why did Laila feel she'd be looked at differently when people knew her upbringing and/or lack of family ties?

3. Should Laila have been more apprehensive about jumping into a relationship when she arrived in Philadelphia?

4. Was Jordan sincere about his reasons for ending the relationship with Laila? Did he really value her friendship?

5. Was the relationship between John and Keisha realistic? What were the pros and cons?

6. Was it a wise decision for Laila to get pregnant?

7. Was John being selfish when Laila asked him to come along to meet her mother?

8. Was Danielle plotting all along?

9. Did John deserve forgiveness?

10. Did Laila appear indebted to David when she returned to Miami?

11. What would you have done differently from Laila when she first met her mother?

12. How will knowing her roots change Laila's future?